MONTANA
Legacy

A Montana Romance

also by velda BROTHERTON

Sexy, Dark, and Gritty.

Twist of Poe Mysteries

The Purloined Skull

The Tell-Tale Stone

The Pit and the Penance

Masque of the Rising Moon

The Victorians

Wilda's Outlaw

Rowena's Hellion

Tyra's Gambler

Other Titles

Beyond The Moon

Remembrance

A Savage Grace

Once There Were Sad Songs

Stoneheart's Woman

Wolf Song

MONTANA *Legacy*

A Montana Romance

VELDA
BROTHERTON

GALWAY

OGHMA CREATIVE MEDIA

www.oghmacreative.com

ISBN: 978-1-63373-239-1

Interior Design by Casey W. Cowan
Editing by Gil Miller

Galway Press
Oghma Creative Media
Bentonville, Arkansas
www.oghmacreative.com

To my friend Pat Richards.

May you rest in peace.

One

The Indian trouble put an end to the range war.

Yancey said it was because of all the activity with the army. The colonel was no fool. He'd bide his time.

Charlie missed Fallon, who'd ridden off soon after he spent the night at her campfire outside Miles City. It surprised her how many times she would look up expecting to see him astride that enormous black stallion of his and be disappointed to find him not there.

The extra hands not needed on the range had built a cookhouse and Crane appeared happily settled in. He'd taken to joining her in the cabin of an evening after supper to talk about Matt and his memories of their childhood. She found herself looking forward to his company.

Even an infestation of screw worms in a herd of cattle on the western range north of the Porcupine didn't cause undue concern. That was just normal to ranch life. Charlie and a few of the men rode out to do some doctoring. The entire month of July had been hot and dry. Rabbit brush and sage crackled beneath the hooves of the ponies as they rode. Several times she raised her face to the blistering wind and thought she smelled smoke, but saw nothing. God help them if the range caught fire in this hot, dry, windy weather.

They worked late into the evening doctoring the cattle, spreading a mixture of axle grease and carbolic acid into the wounds left by the flies that laid their eggs beneath the thick hide of the beasts.

In the midst of choking dust and bawling cattle, Charlie heard the dreaded words "Fire, fire," and felt her stomach clench.

She mounted Belle and quickly scanned the horizon. Hungry flames and a column of smoke to the southwest ran ahead of the wind straight for the herd.

She interrupted the jabbering of the excited hand who had ridden up with the news. "Has it jumped the Yellowstone and the Bighorn?"

The man's eyes were wide with fright. All he wanted to do was get on his horse and ride. She grabbed the horse's bridle. "I asked you—"

The man fairly screamed his answer. "She come right cross the river and ain't nothin' gonna stop her—nothin' in this wide world." He cut at the horse's flanks with his spurs, the jumping animal's shoulder bumped the roan's and she danced nervously.

Charlie calmed Belle and shouted orders. "Listen to me. We can save these cattle, pick up others as we go. Head 'em south and east. We can't outrun it, but we sure as hell can outflank it. The whole world is not on fire—not yet anyway. We'll just run like hell out of its path."

Concern for Yancey claimed her attention. He'd taken some of the men to the north pasture to check on the herd there and could be trapped by the inferno. No time for that worry now.

"Ritter!" She reined in the prancing roan. "Right here."

"Round up as many as you can, let the strays go.

"Flank 'em over there." She pointed, and Ritter took two men and rode. Circling in the opposite direction with three other hands, she rounded up a fair-sized herd and started them moving east. South of the ranch house where the Porcupine bent back to the north and onto the Circle D, they would turn the herd down toward the Yellowstone. If the wind didn't switch, it would wipe out the ranch houses at the Double H, the Rocking R, and maybe even Dunkirk's Circle D, but this herd would be saved.

The half-dozen hands drove the herd hard, down through a draw and over the next ridge. Beyond in a flat meadow, Charlie spotted some more grazing cattle. Each in turn raised their heads to point long spreading horns skyward, bawled, and galloped along with the thundering herd when it overtook them.

They had a jump on the fire, maybe all they needed, and she didn't look back. It took all of her strength not to ride directly to the ranch and try to save the buildings, but she knew that was useless. The wind might shift. Or it might rain. Neither possibility seemed very likely. She tried not to think of Yancey.

Save enough cattle to survive the winter. That's what she had to do, all she could think of doing.

It seemed like an eternity of eating dust before the herd finally reached the Porcupine. The lead cattle slowed, milled in the water till it turned muddy. She drew her rifle and fired several shots in the air. The other hands followed suit and rode into the creek, forcing the cows through.

Ritter caught up with her on the far bank. "Miss Charlie, I believe we're out of its path. Look yonder."

He was right. The fire had continued to move to the northeast. The ravaging beast would miss them, but not the ranch, unless something stopped it.

"Okay, start turning them down toward the Yellowstone," she shouted, and he passed the word.

They were off Double H property. Though Colonel Dunkirk used this land north of Miles City for grazing, he didn't legally own it. He had run ads in *The Post* that he held possessory rights, and that made most believe it was his, but she knew better. All the same the man wouldn't be happy about her putting her cattle there. He was bound to try to do something about it and use the law to back him up.

Soon after they turned the cattle and let them meander into the river to drink, she asked Ritter's help to get a head count.

When they'd finished the tally, Ritter asked, "You reckon Yancey Barton'll see that fire a-comin'?"

"Well, if he don't, he's blind as a shedding snake," one of the hands piped up. "Lookee yonder at her burn."

They paused to stare in awe as flames and smoke highballed it across the dry prairie. Off to her right, crossing the path of that inferno, rose a growing pillar of dust. She scarcely believed what she saw then. A herd of longhorns emerged from waves of summer heat like specters appearing from nowhere. And riding flat out, two horsemen, one on each side.

She lit out in the direction of the galloping herd. "Whoopee. Let's give 'em a hand."

The far rider was Yancey Barton, and coming right at her, covered in dust and bent over in the saddle, rode Mitch Fallon. He looked about as much like a gunslinger as Ritter at that moment. She rode past him to bunch up the rear of the herd, took off her hat and waved it in a circle above her head, shouting an enormous whoppee. His answering yee-hah brought laughter from deep down inside her. It felt good.

The hands at the river helped slow the running cattle with shouts of their own. As they mixed in with Charlie's bunch there was a great deal of celebration among the men.

Charlie held back, embarrassed to approach Fallon who, surprisingly, was right in the middle of the celebration. Instead she dismounted, tied the mare, and walked a ways uphill from the drinking cows to watch the smoke on the horizon race up-country. On its way to the ranch. At least they'd saved some cattle. Others would be spared simply because they were not in the path of the fire.

She didn't look at Fallon until he spoke. "Wind's dropping. If it lays at sundown the fire might burn itself out along the banks of the Porcupine."

She lifted her face into the wind so that it dried the dust-coated sweat. Removing her hat she rubbed gloved fingers through her hair, then peeled off the gloves and doubled them over her belt. She tried every reason she could think of not to look at him, but none of them worked.

He grinned, poked at her cheek with a finger. "Muddy face."

The familiar voice and the tone he used filled her with longing. God, how she'd missed him. "Yours, too," she said, but didn't touch him like he had her.

He quickly pulled his finger away, looked down at his boot toes. "Both could use a wash, I reckon."

What were they doing talking about dirty faces? She thought of plenty of other things she wanted to say, but didn't. They just stood there for a while staring at each other.

Finally he grunted, took off his hat, and blotted at his forehead with one arm. The wind caught at his hair, twisting the white streak through the long dancing tresses.

Peering out of the grime, his eyes gleamed like summer rain, and she couldn't help but remember what it felt like to be in his arms.

"Thought you were gone," she finally managed, but only after she pulled from the trap of that intense gaze to look down the slope at the watering cattle.

"Nope." He put his hands on his hips and that's when she noticed he wasn't wearing the Colt.

"Where's your gun?"

"Been working cattle. Rifle's enough."

She raised her brows. "Oh? For who?"

"Burris needed a hand, thought I'd stick around." "He wasn't afraid to hire you?"

"No, in fact he liked the idea, once I convinced him I no longer rode for the colonel." He grinned again, showing his flashing teeth and erasing the sternness. "Kind of peeved I wouldn't wear the Colt, though. Thought he'd hired him a gunhand."

"Didn't he?"

He was quiet for a while, then turned to stare at her until she finally looked back at him. "Only if needs be. Sometimes any man'll fight, given enough reasons."

"Or woman." Without saying any more, she placed her hat back on her head and left him standing there, hands still on his hips and long legs spread wide in the dusty black britches, hair whipping in the wind. She turned once to look and saw he hadn't watched her walk away, but was gazing out across the prairie.

Like Fallon had predicted the wind laid at dusk. By dark they could see the line of fire stretching for miles, not wild and wicked but burning lazily. They watched until it reached an arroyo, or perhaps the trickle of Porcupine Creek, and then it just burned itself out. Soon the stars were brighter than the dying embers, and there was left only the pungent smoldering odor in the night air.

"Well," one of the hands joked, "I prayed for rain, but guess the Good Lord figured I just didn't know what I was asking for."

Chuckles worked their way around the campfire. Everyone sat on their bedrolls, chewing on jerky or hard biscuits most carried when they were out on the range and conversing in soft voices. Augurin', the old-timers called it.

"Miss Charlie, whyn't you sing us one of your'n Cal's songs?" Ritter asked.

She picked up a stick and drew lines in the dirt. She hadn't sung for anyone but herself since Cal Malone's death. The hands had all at one time or another heard her singing to the cattle as she stood guard, either on the drive up from Texas or out here on the range. Only a few knew Cal wrote the poetry that she put to music.

She began to hum softly and everyone grew quiet. The fire crackled and popped, and off in the distance wolves set up a conversation. She sang them a song about a Montana lady who fell in love with a back east dandy who broke her heart when he went back home to marry his sweetheart. One of the boys accompanied the tune with a mouth harp, hesitantly at first till he got the rhythm, then sweetly, sadly.

A knot formed in her throat as she finished the song. It made her voice husky. "And high on the hill where the wild wind blows, she sits her strawberry roan. And cries to the wolf in the moon's white glow, her heart turned hard as stone."

The plaintive last notes from the mouth harp faded and no one said anything for a long while after the notes died away.

Then Ritter said, "That old Cal, he had him some poet's soul, didn't he?"

Tears surprised Charlie and she wiped them with the heels of her hands. "I think he had Robert Burns memorized."

"Robert Burns?"

"A poet."

"I knew a fella once could quote poetry," someone across the fire said. "But not me. I can't even read it good, too many odd words."

"Them ain't odd words, Quigley, they's just longer than the and but." Everyone chuckled.

She sensed someone moving up on her from out of the dark and swung around. It was Mitchell Fallon, all washed clean, his hair wet and curly around his face. Firelight shone on his high cheeks and broad jaw, reflected in the glade-green eyes. He reached a hand down to her without saying a word and she took it, rising easily to her feet.

The savory tang of burning wood scented the still air. She walked beside him still holding to his hand, and they strolled away from the glow of firelight. Below them the river reflected dancing points of starlight, scattered and blurred as if unreal.

"What will you do?" she finally asked.

His thumb roamed over the back of her hand. "Do?"

"Once the soldiers are gone, the colonel will start up again. He'll fight till he takes all the land away from us. He'll pick us off one at a time till the ones left are too scared to stay and light out. Then, what will you do?"

He tightened his hold on her hand, stopped walking. "I'm not going to let him do that to you." His voice was hard as flint, scary, and she could believe him very easily. He could be a frightening man.

"You mean just to me, or to all of us?"

"I meant you, I guess. It's you I care about."

She looked up at him. "I don't understand why." But inside she did and her heart knocked around like it had broken loose and didn't have a place to go.

He lifted her chin with the other hand, the one he wasn't already holding on to her with, and bent to kiss her gently. She flicked her tongue out to touch his warm lips, surprising him. His eyes widened and he wrapped his arms around her, deepening the kiss.

When they finally pulled part, he said, "Damn if I know what to do about you."

Snaking her arms around his waist she said softly, "There's nothing you can do about me."

He laughed into her hair. "Blamed if that isn't true."

"Come to work for me," she said, and lay her cheek against his chest so she could hear his heart beat. "Together we can make the Double H what Matthew wanted it to be."

"Matthew?"

"My dad. I worked with him so long I just called him Matthew like all the men on his ranch. I was five years old when he put me astride my first horse. Quite a shock to a little girl who'd been raised in drawing rooms wearing stiff dresses and patent leather shoes. But I took to it." She rubbed her cheek against the fabric of his shirt.

"I loved him so much, and you—"

"I am not Matthew, not your father." He stiffened, thinking of a little girl he had failed to protect. A little girl to whom he was a father. "I can't make you any promises, Charlie."

"So far, I haven't asked for any." She felt as if he had struck her, or at the very least withdrawn from her once again.

"But you will. You have to. The only promise I've made was to myself, and that was to see that you don't get hurt. I'll break it only if they kill me."

A chill washed through her. He spoke of his own death so casually. Yet he still held her in his arms, hadn't pushed her away, even though she'd sensed his retreat. "Wouldn't it be easier to keep your promise if you were living on the Double H? The Burns ranch is a long ways off."

"That's why I was on my way back down here when I saw the fire. It occurred to me that I needed to be closer to you."

Charlie wiggled up tight against him, felt his muscles quiver and his arms tighten. "Is this about close enough?" She felt breathless, on the brink of something important and arousing.

Fallon lowered his mouth to the hollow of her throat. She vibrated with desire, slipped her hands up under his shirt.

Beneath her palms his smooth warm flesh pulsed with life, and she wanted him desperately and completely.

"Come, come with me. Hurry," she said breathlessly.

Pulling from his embrace, she took his hand and led him partway down the riverbank to a secluded spot beneath a thick stand of willows. In the dark shadows they were well away from the campfire and the cattle.

Tense and on the edge of a passion that threatened to smother all his senses, he could only think of her naked in his arms, between his legs consuming his urgent need. Yet he knew, back in a dim-lit corner of his mind, that if he did this he was setting his path in a way he might not wish to go. A way in which she might regret going. He could not pledge himself to this woman, yet his desire for her verged on lunacy. He blocked out a dire foreboding from that hidden place where he stored his doubts about life and death, his fears of his own inadequacy.

If she were a man he would know how to handle her. He would pull out his gun and shove the barrel into her soft belly, say leave me be or I'll put a bullet in you.

That's how threatened he felt, yet he wanted her in ways he'd never dreamed of wanting a woman.

She challenged even the most formidable of his resolves.

She dragged him down to the ground. It was so dark he couldn't see her, could only hear her quick breaths, feel her fingers fumbling with the buttons on his shirt, making their way down to his belt buckle.

A white-hot flame of desire grew everywhere she touched him, and he helped her loosen his pants. They were both on their knees, her head bent so that fine strands of her hair tangled with the dark curls on his chest.

He captured her hands in his for a moment to give him time. Time to calm the wild surge of passion. Time to make sense out of this unexpected fierce tenderness uncoiling like a sleeping beast within him. He had thought love gone from him forever. Where had this come from, this renewed perception of self and needs and caring, of life itself?

"Charlie, Charlie, are you sure?" He could scarcely breathe out the question for fear she'd say no, for fear she'd say yes.

She answered him in a fierce whisper. "I'm sure. I've waited so long, and you're going to go away. If I don't love you, if you don't love me now, you'll be gone and I'll never—you'll never—we won't know what it would have been like. What it will be like. I just want to love you. One time. I just want you to love me. One time. Then it won't matter, nothing will. Because I'll know. Don't you see? We'll both know forever and always what it was like to be so totally absorbed with such—such freedom of spirit, such ecstasy.

"So, do love me. Please do."

She wrung her hands free of his grasp, tugged at his pants, got them open and down past his hipbones. She lowered her head and kissed his belly button. Her tongue darted out, flicking at his quivering flesh like little bites from the sun.

He tried to reason with her, senseless words that climbed from coarse to ragged, but she wouldn't stop unless he hurt her and he couldn't do that. So he lay down on the ground as she lowered his britches over his hips and spreading his hands at her waist lifted her so that she straddled his thighs.

She still wore her clothes and felt awkward sitting on him that way. Rising to her knees she began to undo her pants.

"No, wait. Wait a minute," he said.

"I can't. I want you... want you inside me. You do, too, I can tell." She squirmed around on his bulging manhood, teasing just a bit, but nevertheless very serious about her intent, plucking and tugging to get rid of the jeans she wore.

He dragged in a deep, jagged breath. "I do, yes, I do. But what you said. You're right about what may happen. I run away. I like to run away when things get too tough. And Charlie Houston, you're too tough."

Softly, "I'm not so tough," then she went on with renewed vigor, "well, anyway, we agreed. It won't matter, we'll know what it's like to love one another. We can keep the memory forever."

"We didn't agree on anything. And this isn't loving one another. This is—well, this is..." He grabbed her with both hands, pulled her head down to his chest and held her tight, his voice hoarse, raw with desire. God, how he wanted her. This very minute. He imagined plunging into her, the hot wet silkiness, the burning, pounding surging release. "This is not what you deserve. You deserve a man who will stick with you, love you, and take care of you."

"No, dammit," she cried and tried to shove away. "I don't need someone to take care of me, I need someone to love me."

Fighting her, holding her. "Okay, okay." Suddenly he was quiet, hugging her close and breathing against her cheek. "It's not me, Charlie. I'm sorry, it's not me." He closed his eyes, wanted to cry for the loss of all he wanted, but it was better. Better to lose it now while he could still bear it.

She hammered at his chest. "Damn you, damn you," she cried, then tore from his arms and leaped to her feet. Infuriated, depleted, she stumbled away from him.

After a while he rolled to his knees, pulled his pants on, and fumbled around in the dark until he found his hat. Pain so intense it took away his breath cracked through him like rage, and he knew all about that. Rage he could deal with and he fed it with every vengeful thought he could muster.

Fallon stayed on at the Double H Ranch, and Charlie tried to pretend she didn't notice. She wanted him to leave, wanted him to stay, did nothing about either, for she couldn't look into his eyes or speak to him for fear the pain would kill her. Yancey finally came to Charlie about him.

"This new hand, this Fallon, when did you hire him?"

A hand squeezed at her heart and she gasped, looked away from Yancey's squinty gaze. "I didn't, not really."

"Then what's he doing sleeping and eating here?"

Lips dry, tongue sticking to the roof of her mouth, she managed, "Is he working?" "I reckon. He just kind a pitches in when something needs done. I ain't never told him to do anything. It's a strange situation, if you don't mind my saying so."

"You don't have to tell me it's strange." If he knew the truth, this friend, what would he then think?

"You want, I can get rid of him. He did work for the colonel, you know. Strange how he just sort of showed up." At that Yancey eyed her in his thoughtful way, and almost grinned, like he knew a secret she might wish to be let in on.

She wanted to tell him it wasn't what he thought at all. "What did you say to him... when he just kind of showed up?"

Yancey scratched up under his hat. "What do you mean, what did I say?"

"Well, I mean when we hire someone new, don't you introduce him around, show him his bunk, tell him his job? You don't just let him sort of fall into things, do you?"

"Not generally. But I have to admit, that's what I did with this fella. He's the falling in kind of man, you know. He acted like he knew where he wanted to sleep and where he wanted to work, and so I figured you'd hired him. I just let him."

"Without even asking me. Sounds like just about anyone could ride in off the trail and go to work here without either one of us hiring him."

Yancey laughed. "Well, now, Miss Charlie, not many men

would just ride up and go to work like this one did. To tell you the truth, this is the first time it's ever come up in all my years of ramrodding for your daddy or even before."

She couldn't help chuckling, though bitterly. It was an unusual situation, and if she hadn't been so blindly furious at Fallon for rejecting her advances, she might have seen even more humor in it. As it was, whether she liked it or not, the Double H had a new hand, and she'd just have to learn to live with that. She certainly wasn't up to confronting him about it. Be damned if she'd tell Yancey to take care of it. He'd think she wasn't up to really running the ranch, just like some of the men already thought.

The best she could do was discuss her pent-up feelings with Radine every chance she had to go to Miles City. They had become friends, and she guessed that's what friends did. Share their innermost secret feelings and desires.

Two

Fallon waited until the lamp went out in Charlie's cabin to assure himself that she had retired for the night, then he came out onto the porch of the bunkhouse. It was a bright night and he had no desire to let anyone see him.

Crane had snuck off earlier, and he intended to catch him coming back, find out what the hell the man was up to. He didn't trust him and his sneaky ways, and he particularly didn't like the way he nosed up to Charlie all the time. Since seeing him meet up with Cross in secret that night in the clearing, he had kept a close eye on the man. He was definitely up to something, and it didn't bode well for Charlie Houston.

Wasn't the cook supposed to be her cousin or something?

It was a long time before Crane returned. Fallon snoozed sitting slumped against a porch post, hat tilted down over his eyes to keep out the bright moonlight. He heard the soft clop of hooves, though, and was instantly alert. Crane came into the brightly lit yard leading his horse slowly to make as little noise as possible. His furtiveness was evident in the way he took his mount into the barn and unsaddled him, came back out a few moments later after having turned the horse into the corral out back.

Stretching lazily, Fallon rose, but Crane didn't see him until he had started up the steps to the bunkhouse.

"Evening, friend," Fallon said.

Crane yipped, sounding just like a dog that had been kicked. He recovered quickly. "What do you mean, scaring a man like that? Good thing for you I don't carry a side arm, I'd a shot you for a thief."

"Or maybe I'd a shot you," Fallon said, his hand going unconsciously to his bare hip. The Colt lay stored in the chest at the foot of his bunk, his way of divorcing himself from the gunhand Charlie knew him to be.

"Don't know why you'd want to do that."

"Oh, I don't know. A man rides out in secret, sneaks back in the wee hours of the night, making sure no one sees him. Must be up to no good of some kind, I'd wager. What would you think?" Fallon slouched against the post, glaring at Crane but unable to see his expression in the shadow cast by his hat.

"I'd think that it was his business entirely, what a man does on his own time." "Unless that business has to do with betraying the brand he rides for."

Crane jerked as if he'd been socked. "Why would you think that? You crazy or something? I love Miss Charlie—hell, she's my own cousin.

"If anybody'd be up to no good around here, I'd guess it'd be you. Come riding in here with a gun on your hip shooting up the place, and next thing we know you're riding herd over Double H cattle. Now, I don't know about some, but I take that as mighty suspicious."

Fallon straightened. Crane had leaned forward so that he felt the heat and moisture of his breath as he spat out the last words. Fallon definitely didn't like anyone coming that close to him, but he'd be damned if he'd back off. "Move away, mister."

The old savagery rose in Fallon's chest but he held back. Charlie might not understand if he maimed her cook. He'd heard the stories of her cooking escapades. Anyone who shot down a perfectly good cook, and on the steps of her bunkhouse to boot, would not be held in very high esteem by Charlie Houston. In fact, she might do some disabling of her own.

Crane shrunk away when he caught sight of the dark figure on the porch.

Fallon grabbed his arm. "I want to tell you something. I can't figure what you and that bastard Cross are up to, but you do anything to hurt Charlie Houston and you've got me to deal with. It won't be pretty, but I promise you this, it'll be quick. Got that?"

A ray of moonlight on Crane's cheek cast great dark hollows around his eyes when he stared up into Fallon's face. His voice trembled when he spoke, but he got the words out. "I don't know what you think you're gonna do with her, but you can be assured no Houston would have any dealings with the likes of you. She'd die first. Now, take your hand off me and let me pass."

Fallon felt the man's arm quiver under his grasp, but he let him go. He had some grit, and that worried him, for in a pinch he might actually show enough courage to do whatever it was he and Cross had planned. He'd have to keep a real good eye on this one. To discover a wolf living in your midst didn't bode well for survival, especially if other wolves were circling to attack.

Fallon waited until all sounds of Crane's retiring were silenced, then he went inside. Before crawling into his own bunk he retrieved the Colt and slipped it under his pillow.

Something awoke Charlie in the predawn hours. She suspected it was only the excitement of fall roundup beginning. After tossing in the bed awhile, she got up and dressed. She would sleep better on the trail, and there was no point in fighting the restlessness any longer.

She stepped out on the porch and dragged in a deep, sweet breath. Birds waking in the brush along the perimeter of the yard warbled inquisitive soft music in the predawn air. A tingle of excitement walked up her spine and radiated across her shoulders. Roundup, the most exciting time of the year.

Crane came down the steps from the porch, didn't see her, and headed for the cookhouse to make breakfast. It wasn't long before the smell of burning wood from his fire tinged the first pale glow of morning.

The place came suddenly alive as if someone had rung bells or blown wake-up call on a horn.

She watched the men and their good-natured horseplay around the washpans for a few moments, then started across the wide yard. She could smell bacon frying and bread baking and so wasn't paying much attention to where she was going. That's how Fallon got right up on her without her seeing him. Or at least, that's what she told herself later. Her hunger had let down the careful guard she'd put up against him ever since that night on the riverbank when he'd refused her advances.

He swept off his black hat, a little the worse for wear since he'd started cowboying.

She guessed gunslingers weren't as hard on their clothes as cowboys, for since he'd taken up the latter occupation his jeans had become worn, his shirt faded, and the boots well used. He looked not at all like he had the first day she'd seen him, all dressed in black sitting atop that prancing stallion, so remote, so fascinating. She stopped and faced him, her chin up so she could look into his face.

"Good morning, Miss Charlie. Looks like you're ready for roundup." He didn't sound cheerful, exactly, but he sounded different than he used to. A little less threatening, and more relaxed. That was the only word she could think of. Relaxed. Like he enjoyed what he was doing.

Well, maybe he did. She'd give him that. She smiled at him, determined to enjoy this day to its fullest. "Good morning to you, Mr. Fallon. I hope you're as ready as I am. I expect my men to work till they drop, just like I will."

She laid a heavy accent on "my men," and looked him right in the eye, no matter that it cost her. A shiver of delight coursed through her when he met her gaze with a smoky one of his own.

"I'll do my best to keep up with you, boss." Fallon screwed the hat back down on his head, cocking it slightly so that it shadowed the scar above his eyebrow.

She didn't notice until he walked away that he had strapped the Colt .44 back on his right hip, low and ready, just like he'd worn it the first time she ever saw him.

Mitch had never ridden a roundup as a cowpuncher, but he had no intentions of sitting this one out. Wherever Charlie was he intended to be, too, and he especially intended to keep an eye on Crane Houston.

The black took well to hard riding, so Mitch set a fast pace to keep up with the other drovers. Yancey had seen to spare mounts for the Double H men and they joined those from other ranches behind the chuck wagon in the care of a wrangler. Whatever job a man was assigned, there'd be a horse trained to do it. His stallion didn't exactly qualify as a cow pony. By the end of a punishing day's ride, the caravan of men and horses and equipment reached its destination.

The rolling land, dotted with spruce and pine, roughened in places into canyons, and it was in one of these that the herd would be held during the process of gathering the scattered cattle.

Mitch could see the reasoning as soon as the wagon boss and his circle riders began to lay out plans for the next day's roundup.

The "canyon," if it could be called that, had a wide, flat entrance with plenty of grass and was flanked by brushy hills. At the other end it narrowed and became boulder-strewn and rough, forming a natural corral big enough to hold all the cattle they'd gather from these sections.

Obviously they'd used the place before.

Crane immediately went about setting up the chuck wagon beneath some lodge pole pines well clear of the entrance to the holding pen. The bed wagon was parked alongside. Several springs fed a small creek nearby and plenty of deadwood lay scattered about.

Luke Awhile, the wrangler from the Bar S, would also hold that job for the roundup. He corralled the remuda of more than a hundred horses and started gathering wood for the cook fire. Assigned all the chores the real cowboys were loathe to do, such as hauling wood and water and cook's helper, Luke could expect to be razzed by the cowboys. They didn't disappoint him.

"Hey, Luke," one of the men hollered at him, "don't you go picking up one of them cow chips afore you check under it. Scorpions do love to bed down in that stuff."

A round of laughter followed as Luke went to work turning over the dried cow chips left from spring roundup to use in the fire.

Fallon remained aloof from the horseplay, preferring to unsaddle his stallion and give him a good rubdown in privacy. He was surprised that the colonel hadn't sent Cross and Neddy to ride along and be their usual troublesome selves, but they were conspicuously absent. Some of the Circle D's regular cowboys eyed Fallon suspiciously. The colonel would soon know that he was riding for the Double H brand, if he didn't already.

That evening he took his tin plate of stew and cup of coffee to a spot where he could keep an eye on just about everyone, most especially Charlie.

The object of his attention stood in line at the chuck wagon with the rest of the men and then took her steaming plate to a table-size boulder a ways back from the campfire. Some of the men gathered in groups, others paired up, and she listened in perfect contentment to their joshing and teasing. This was what she liked best about ranching. The roundups, the getting out and riding free and shouting into the wind and sleeping under a raven-black sky sprinkled with stars.

It was at times like this that she missed her father the most, and feeling a little lonely, she finished her meal. After scraping the last few bites of stew out of her plate on the ground for the night critters she took her dinnerware to the washtub where the jingler would scrub everything clean before retiring for the night. As she turned and started around the back end of the chuck wagon, she spied a lone figure at the crest of the rise, a dark silhouette against the silvery evening sky. Standing out there staring down at the campfire, alone and removed from everyone, he made her think of how she'd been feeling herself. Someone else lonely like her. The sight brought a thickening to her throat.

She wanted—*she* wanted *something*, an unnamed something, and seeing that singular cowboy outlined against the fading daylight made her almost sick with the need for a thing she couldn't even put a name to. She climbed the rise toward the man. She'd speak, remark on the day, talk about tomorrow, and if he didn't respond, well then she could always walk away. It was possible that he wasn't lonely at all, but simply wanted privacy, in which case she would leave him alone.

As she approached the mysterious figure, he turned to stare out across the valley, and too late she realized that it was Mitch

Fallon. She should have known. He never took up with anyone, always set himself apart. Well, perhaps she had known it was him and chose this way to break the long silence that had held between them since that fateful night on the riverbank.

"Beautiful, isn't it?" Surely she could have thought of something better to say.

"Yes, it is beautiful, but only when it sleeps."

"I heard you coming, wondered if you'd hightail it when you figured out who I was."

"Why should I run from you? I'm not afraid of you. What do you mean, only when it sleeps?"

"Life here. It's so harsh that sometimes the beauty gets lost in the demands the land makes on us, in our striving to endure. Sometimes it's just so damned hard to get from one day to the next that nothing is beautiful enough."

"That sounds like self-pity to me," she snapped, angry at him and not sure why.

He snorted but didn't reply right away. Charlie was afraid he'd hear the thumping of her heart, and wondered why she couldn't be anywhere near him without feeling tumultuous and giddy.

He finally spoke, so softly she had to strain to hear him. "I guess it does. I just don't know how to get on with it, and so sometimes I get to feeling sorry for myself. I know I'm not different from lots of others who've lost all they love, but that doesn't make it any easier."

She scarcely breathed as he talked, for he had never spoken in such revealing terms to her. She wanted him to go on, let her inside the world in which he survived so tenaciously, so angrily.

He startled her then by turning grasping her upper arms, and looking down into her face. "I couldn't save her, no matter what I did or how hard I tried. And you're as stubborn as she was. But I will not let anything happen to you. I promise you that."

Then he turned her loose as if she were a demon, and before she could react at all, he strode away. She wanted to go after him, make him explain what he meant, make him talk to her so she could learn what kind of man this was. But she couldn't move from the spot, and so she stood there rubbing her arms where he had held her. And she watched him until his shadow blended with the other shadows in the canyon. It was like watching him disappear off the face of the earth. She wanted to howl like the coyotes off in the distance. Howl and howl until Fallon turned and answered, came to her call and carried her off somewhere and they could make love in the woods like wild things until she would at last be sated. And maybe he would tell her what he was all about.

By dawn the next morning the wagon boss had left with a dozen circle riders. They would remain in the saddle eighteen out of twenty-four hours driving cattle from their assigned sections for miles around.

Though Charlie wasn't a circle rider, she did work the herds all day, and took her turn nighthawking as well. She had chosen her favorite roan Belle for that task, leaving some of the less surefooted animals for day work. She and the little roan got along well, they understood each other because they'd always been together. Matt had given her the foal even as it stood wobbly and wet at its mother's side. She had broken Belle herself, and loved her as only a young woman without friends can come to love a pet, with all her heart and soul.

The wolves came on the fifth night, spooking first the horses in their rope corral, and eventually the longhorns. The pack dashed and darted at the fringes of the herd, picking calves as their natural target. Before anyone could react the cows began to mill and bawl, tossing their heads so their immense horns cracked together like rifle shots.

She and Belle had started around the wide mouth of the canyon when the remuda began to cut up. Belle lifted her ears, snorted, and whinnied. Charlie swung her around so that she was facing the milling cattle straight on, and in the same instant came the ominous low rumble as the cattle started to move. Back deep in the herd, waves of panic spread outward, like rocks tumbling into an avalanche.

She stuck her spurs in hard and got the roan out of the way of the chaos, then rode hard alongside, anxious to contain the stampede, put a stop to it quickly. Other night riders did the same.

The ground shook like thunder. Charlie bent low over the roan's neck, heard the valiant horse's breath chuffing in and out as she raced to outdistance the cattle so they could be turned in upon themselves.

In the darkness she made out shadowy clumps of boulders as she and the horse raced through the night. Cowboys yipped, and it sounded as if someone had reached the front of the herd, for several shots resounded from that direction. They were ahead and trying to turn the lead cattle, stop the stampede.

She blanked out memories of another stampede, lightning and pouring rain, balls of dancing fire and death. Matt's death. She mustn't think of anything but stopping the herd. Hooves pounded, dust boiled, her heart kept a beat with the cacophony, and then the cattle turned, swinging around so that she and the roan were caught in the center of the vortex.

The drovers must not see her, must not know she was there.

The roan screamed, shuddered, and screamed again, then went down into the maelstrom of pounding hooves and bawling, panicking cattle.

Kicking free of the stirrups, Charlie bounced literally onto the heaving back of a broad-shouldered steer, slid down his side, and was swallowed up by the herd. She rolled into a ball, tucked her head low, and covered it with both arms. A sharp hoof cut into her thigh, another kicked her into a tumble among the churning legs.

Involved in a nightmare of choking dust and the stink of fear, she only had time to think how ironic that she should die in the same way her father had, before strong arms swept her up and out of the deadly stampede.

Wild with fear for her life, Fallon had urged the powerful black right into the herd as soon as he saw her go down. The cattle were turning, slowing, and God help him, maybe he could get to her in time.

He kept thinking over and over. Get to her, get to her, save her, for God's sake.

And then he had a firm hold on her, swooping her up off the ground and into the saddle before him like a bundle of rags. By that time the cattle were no longer in headlong flight, but still confused and very dangerous. The black shouldered his way through them as if born to the task, escaping with only a shallow gash across one shoulder.

At first Fallon couldn't tell if Charlie was breathing, or if she was all broken up, the life stomped out of her. He carried her to the campfire, where the cowboys gathered around, murmuring among themselves, some shocked and totally mute. Yancey tried to take her from his arms, but Fallon just kept walking, his features like hard cut stone, his eyes haunted.

Ritter and Crane made her a bed near the fire where they could tend to her wounds and Fallon put her there, but he wouldn't release her hand, and they had to work around where he knelt beside her, the limp hand clasped against his chest. None dared challenge the warning in his glittering eyes. Crane, charged with administering first aid as the cook usually was, brought out his box of supplies and went to work cleaning the blood and dirt from her face. Immediately she began to make mewling sounds down in her throat, and Fallon lifted her hand to his mouth, bending over it to taste the reassuring warmth.

If she died—no, he wouldn't let himself think such a thing. If she lived, that's what he would think. If she lived, he promised her in silence, if she would just live he would take her in his arms and make love to her, just like she had wanted. My God, how could he have denied her and himself that? Life was so fleeting, death so furtive and sneaky. He should have learned that by now.

No, dammit, no, he would not let her die.

He rocked on his knees. "Don't die, don't die," he whispered against the battered knuckles of her fingers.

She stirred, moaned, and began to thrash around.

"Hold her still," Crane ordered, and Fallon took her by the shoulders. Ritter captured her legs and stopped her from flailing. "Don't feel like any ribs are broken," Crane announced. He went on to check her entire body with capable hands, acting as if he knew what he was doing. By the time he finished, looking a bit chagrined because this was a woman he was laying hands on, Charlie had fully regained consciousness.

The first face she looked into was Fallon's, because he still hovered over her, refusing to move. Crane simply had to do his doctoring around him, and so that's what he did, him not being the kind to confront a man who held death by such a loose rein.

Eyes going wide and rolling, Charlie screamed, "Matt, Matt, no."

"Ssh, ssh, you're fine," Fallon whispered. He cupped her face with both hands to stop her throwing her head back and forth. "Charlie, everything's okay."

His breath exploded out of him with relief as he uttered the words. Yet he worried.

She could be hurt inside, and they wouldn't know it right

away. She really should be checked out for wounds all over her body. He rose and bellowed at the gathered, worried faces.

"Git. All of you git. Can't you see we need to give her some privacy. Go on."

The men darted glances at Yancey and at the wagon boss, who had come in during the melee. Both nodded. They understood that this woman couldn't be stripped naked in front of everyone. They all pulled back into the shadows, turning away as if ashamed.

Fallon leaned down over her and began to unbutton her shirt. "Goddammit, why didn't you stay where you belonged?" He spoke so softly that only she heard him, if she was capable yet of understanding what was being said.

Her eyes shifted quickly back and forth, then lit on him and stayed there a moment. She frowned in puzzlement and formed a name with her lips, but he couldn't tell what it was. Surely not his.

"You know, a doctor ought to see her," Crane said to Yancey so that Fallon could hear.

"I agree," Yancey said.

"'No, no. I'm okay," Charlie said very clearly.

She struggled to sit up, but Fallon held her down, pulled the shirt back to inspect for bruises, swelling, and breaks in the skin.

Yancey stepped forward. "I'm not sure you ought to be doing that," he told Fallon.

Fallon glared at him, slid his spread hands beneath her rib cage to feel around on her back. She strained to sit up.

"No, no, not yet, just lay there," he murmured. "Do you hurt anywhere?" She chuckled grimly. "I hurt everywhere."

After checking her neck, back, and front, Fallon reached for the buckle on her belt. "And it's bound to get worse, too. I'm just going to take a look at your stomach, okay?"

She gazed up at him a moment, then nodded. Yancey sighed in disgust.

Fallon slipped her pants down past her hips and palpated her stomach gently with the tips of his fingers. "Tell me if it hurts."

She nodded, watching him, lower lip caught in her teeth.

Ritter stood a few feet away, watching without embarrassment. "I'm riding to the ranch to get the buckboard."

Yancey blew out an explosive breath and turned away from the sight of the gunslinger with his hands all over Charlie. "Good idea," he told Ritter. "We're closer to the Rocking R. Cal's buckboard should still be in his barn, no reason for it not to be. Take two horses out of the remuda. We'll try to keep her down till you get back."

Ritter nodded, stared worriedly down at Charlie for a few seconds, then took off on a run. "I'll be back by dawn."

"Belle, where is she?" Charlie asked hoarsely.

Fallon, who had found a blanket to cover her with after he removed her jeans, pulled it up under her chin and swung around to stare toward the distant spot where he'd pulled her from the trampling hooves. No one had thought about her horse.

She grabbed his arm. "Don't let her suffer, please."

"I won't. I'll go see to her right now."

"Please do. Please." There were tears in her voice, choking her.

He pulled his Winchester out of the scabbard and walked the quarter mile or so to where the roan lay. He needed the break, time to think about what had almost happened to Charlie, and to him, too. The walk out and back would give him that. Help him settle some of his rocketing emotions. When he reached the forlorn lump in the churned-up grass he saw immediately that there was no need for a bullet, the little horse was dead. Poor Charlie, he'd seen how she loved that roan, and he hated like hell to tell her Belle was gone.

On the way back to the campfire he got to thinking about how he'd worried that the colonel would send someone to hurt Charlie. All the time it would be something else that would bring her down, something no one could have prevented. A cowboy riding herd expected to one day be killed in a stampede, or gored or stomped or flung off a cliff in some wild night ride. Death came on many feet, it only seemed more tragic when man added to the risk by doing some killing of his own.

She appeared to be sleeping when he returned, so he took the black to the rope corral and spent some time rubbing him down after he pulled off the saddle. The grooming kept his mind and hands occupied, but it also gave him time to think about how he felt. So much had changed for him since he rode down out of Canada scarcely two years ago so his wife could visit with her people. Perhaps the biggest change, though, had occurred right here on this range after he met Charlie Houston. For before that all he'd wanted was to die. Now all he wanted was for her to live.

He strode back to where she lay and knelt beside her. "You can't die on me." He grazed his fingertips over her forehead and down one cheek. "I won't let you."

Her eyelids fluttered and she looked up at him out of those ebony eyes. "Did you take care of Belle?"

"Yes, yes I did. Everything's okay now."

She let her eyes drift shut, and he bent to kiss her tenderly, first on one cheek, then the other. "I love you, Charlie Houston. I just hope I have the courage to tell you when you can hear me, when we can do something about it."

He fetched a blanket and lay down nearby where he could keep an eye on her until Ritter returned with the wagon. He would be going back to Miles City with her.

Three

Mae and Lige Sample, owners of the general mercantile, put Charlie up in their spare room right down the street from the doctor's place. When she'd been in bed four days she decided enough was enough. Everyone was at roundup except her and Fallon, who hovered around her like an old setting hen.

Stretching her sore legs gingerly beneath the covers, she smiled at visions of him sitting beside her, holding her hand as if she might break. With a grunt born of exasperation at being bedridden, she threw off the covers and eased both legs over the edge of the bed. The flannel nightgown hitched up over her knees as she slid forward.

At that instant there came a rap-rap on the door and it swung open. Fallon stood there, hat in both hands, gaping at her. "What in thunder do you think you're doing?" He came across the room in two great strides and plucked her up into his arms just as she hefted herself to her feet.

"Never mind what I'm doing, what do you think you're doing?" she replied. "Hmmm," he said, and nuzzled her neck.

"Fallon, stop that. What in the world has gotten into you?" Despite her protest, she thoroughly enjoyed being held in his arms. His energy and vibrant masculinity gave her strength. She purely tingled with anticipation.

"As I recall," he said into her ear, "you once wanted me to do more than this." "Don't remind me." She locked her arms around his neck, concentrated on the clean line of his full lips for a long moment, and then kissed him softly.

He responded by opening his mouth in welcome, but she had pulled away already. "Now put me down before you bring disgrace on my head."

At that moment, with Fallon nibbling at her ear and making silly animal noises that she protested to only meekly, Mae Sample bustled into the room. Because she was carrying a clean towel and washcloth with a bar of soap balanced on top in one hand and a pitcher of water in the other, she was almost across the room before she noticed the hanky-panky going on right under her nose.

"Oh. Oh, my. Well, I do declare. I mean, what is the meaning of this, sir?" The soap plunked to the floor, followed by the towel and washcloth and a big dollop of water from the brimming pitcher. "Dear me, oh, dear me."

"Fallon," Charlie warned sternly.

Laughing, he set her down on the bed and recovered the items from the floor, presenting them to Mae Sample with a broad bow. Then he retrieved his hat where it had fallen to the floor when he entered, held it poised above his head, flashed a smile, and said, "Ladies, good afternoon," and left.

Charlie stared after him, her mouth hanging open.

"Are you all right, Miss Houston?" Mae asked, so flustered she had turned beet-red beneath her fuzz of graying hair.

"Yes, of course I am. Mr. Fallon is—well, he's quite exuberant at times. He doesn't mean anything by it."

"Probably didn't have a proper raising," Mae muttered. "But that's no call to act so ungentlemanly. The very idea, entering your room and you in only your nightclothes.

Let alone…well, I mean…did he have you in his arms?" Mae patted at her bun, tried to tame the escaping frizz.

Charlie muffled a giggle. "I don't think so, no," she lied. "He was just helping me. I'm going to get out of bed today so I can go home, and he was just—just—" She let it drop, for she could tell by the woman's expression she was getting nowhere.

It occurred to her that she was acting pretty silly herself, giggling and making excuses for her actions like some schoolgirl. That was not at all like her.

She hugged herself. She could still feel his arms around her, pressed up against his chest, the beating of his heart, thump-thumping against her breast, his warm, sweet breath feathering her tingling skin.

Oh, dear God, Fallon, where will we go from here?

The practical answer, of course, was nowhere. To leave it be would be best. But she didn't feel very practical. In fact, she felt flushed, excited, expectant. She had asked him to make love to her once and he had refused. What would he do if she made that same request again? More importantly, would she ask again now that it clearly would mean commitment?

When it was time to leave Fallon embarrassed her by carrying her out of the Samples' front door, down the path, and into the street where he placed her with a flourish on the wagon seat. "Would you rather ride lying down?" he asked.

"No, no, this is fine," she replied and smoothed her skirts. Skirts. Ye Gods, the man was mad. He'd gone to Sample's mercantile and bought her a dress to go home in, and she had put it on, fingers trembling as she buttoned the smooth fabric up over her breasts. Of course, he hadn't thought to bring her a corset and Mae had come running over with one, along with a chemise when she'd learned what was going on. And long stockings and lace-up shoes. Lord, her feet ached already, longed for the supple leather of her well-worn boots. She'd begged him to let her wear the boots under the dress, but he was having none of it and had already bundled her slightly tattered things and put them in the buckboard.

She waited until they were well out of Miles City on the way back to the ranch before she tackled him.

"All right. I want an explanation, now while we're alone and you can't go running off when the questions get too hard."

"All what?" He slapped the reins smartly on the horses' rumps so that they broke into a trot.

"This"—she gestured at the dress—"and this," she said and puckered up her lips to make a loud kissing sound. "All of it. I think you know exactly what."

"Are you angry?" He angled a glance at her, saw she was hanging on and making faces, and slowed the team. "Are you sure you don't need to lie down in the back?"

"I'm fine. Just fine. Thank you for slowing down, though. My tail is still sore."

"Oh, Charlie. Dress you like a lady and you still talk like a—"

"Talk like a *what*? I talk like Charlie Houston, not some simpering city-bred female."

"Okay, okay. You're right. I love you the way you are."

"Then why in thunder did you make me get all gussied up in this—this—oh, God, I can't breathe. How do women wear this getup? No wonder they get the vapors all over the place all the time." Suddenly she stopped chattering and stared at him. "Wait, wait. You love me? Is that what you said?"

He nodded and grinned, turning to look at her adoringly. "Stop this wagon, this instant," she said.

"What? Now, right here?"

She looked around. "Well, no, up there in those trees." "Yes, ma'am," he said.

"And don't—"

"—call you ma'am?"

Neither of them spoke again until he had pulled the wagon deep in the stand of spruce.

Without the protest of the wagon wheels, the clanging and rattling of the double tree, the day was peaceful. Birds chattered among themselves high in the trees and a soft breeze touched at Charlie's loose hair, blowing a strand across her cheek.

He slid over toward her, slipped off his glove, and twisted the fine hair in his fingers. "Beautiful, the way you let it blow loose like that. Not all knotted up on your head like you're ashamed of it or something. It shines like polished wood."

"Fallon," she said softly, and turned so she could kiss the inside of his wrist. "I want to love you. I *do* love you."

She blinked her eyes, surprised that a tear slid from beneath one lid and ran slowly down her cheek.

"Aw, don't cry." He put a finger at her jawline, caught the tear, and put it between his lips. "I don't want to hurt you."

"You aren't *hurting* me."

"I guess I never understood why a woman cries when she does." "It's okay if you don't understand, as long as you care."

"I care, darlin'. I do care."

"Let's go home, then. Now. I've got to get out of these clothes and back to work. I'm going to Cheyenne with the herd."

Fallon's mouth dropped open. "You're not." Not really an order, but more a statement of amazed disbelief.

She tilted her head and smiled sweetly. "Yes, I am. You might as well learn before we even start this, and I am anxious to start, you know." She took one of his suspended hands in both of hers. "I'm not going to do what some man tells me. For too long I've made up my own mind. Matt believed every full-grown person had that right, and so do I."

For a long moment he was totally speechless. Finally he let loose on her. "I'm not 'some man.' And you were just dragged from under the hooves of stampeding cattle.

Someone has to have some common sense. How can you think of making that ride so soon?"

"It'll be a few weeks before the herd is ready to go. By then I'll be fine. I've looked forward to going all summer, and I'm going. I hope you'll come along, too. But not to take care of me."

"Not to take care of you," he repeatedly woodenly. "I can still see you bouncing around in the dirt under all those cows like some danged rag doll, all limp and looking dead."

"Oh, I know." She kissed the hand she held, leaned her head on his arm. "You saved my life and I'm grateful. But not because you're a man and I'm a woman.

Because you saw someone in trouble and you helped out. Anyone would do the same for a friend. I mean...well, you know what I mean."

This time he couldn't say anything. He squeezed his eyes closed, hoping the visions wouldn't come, but they did. Celia being kicked over and over by the vicious boots of her attackers. The baby, strapped to her back, cries cut off brutally before he could reach them. Then, abruptly, Charlie lying wan and still on the blanket beside the fire, and him thinking she would die.

"No, I won't. Dammit, no. I can't." His stern denial cut hard into the soft summer air, his fists clenched until cords stood out in both arms. "This will not happen, I won't let it."

She stiffened, shoved herself out of his reach, but he only smashed at the buckboard seat, hitting it with one fist, then the other. The sharp thunks echoed off across the valley. A flock of birds rose from the nearby trees like a twisting cloud, squawking into the blue sky.

For a brief instant she had thought he would hit her.

Maybe it was the granite set of his rugged features, or the shadows that clouded his green eyes. Whatever it was, her heart had leaped into her throat and she threw her hands up to ward off the expected blows.

The gesture registered belatedly, and he touched her arm gently with the back of one hand. She jerked involuntarily.

Without a word, he unwound the heavy leather reins from around the brake lever and set the team in motion. They must have gone five miles before he spoke in a deadly flat tone. "I just can't watch another woman I love die and not able to do anything about it. You belong in the kitchen, in the bedroom, in my arms—not out taking your life in your hands every day."

Miserable, she nodded. She understood why he felt the way he did, yet wasn't able to agree to such a thing. "And you? I can sit at home and wait for someone to shoot you down because you wear that dreadful gun hanging on your hip. Or maybe you'll get ground to bits under a stampeding herd and it's okay if I have to wait for that to happen. What's the difference? Tell me, please. What's the difference?"

He shook his head, glowering. "I wouldn't have hit you, you know. Back there. You were afraid."

She bit her lip, admitted it. "Yes, for just a split second, I thought you would. Some men do things like that to women."

"Not this man."

"But how could I know? We don't know each other yet. It takes time, and I want us to have that time. But not if you're going to tell me what I can do. Not if you're going to try to change me from what I am, from what you love, into something I'm not. Into a pampered, protected little helpless female. If you can't make peace with that, well, I'm sorry.

"You said you loved me." The last she uttered in such a forlorn voice that he turned to her.

"Oh, God, I do. You don't know how much. I love you more than anything in this world or the next. I cherish you. More than the breath I draw, all that out there, the sky, the sun, the wind. If I had more words I would use them. I can't even tell you how much I love you because not all the words have been invented for that. You are why I am still alive, do you know that?"

"And you are why I'm still alive, Mitch, and I do know that. You literally dragged me away from death's reach, and I was so afraid until I felt your arms I thought I would die of the fright, even if those cows didn't kill me."

"Then why?"

"Because I won't hide from life anymore. I think...well, I guess I really do know that after my father was killed I hunkered down into this little dark place where nothing could get to me. I was too tough, mean sometimes. Hard, so hard. But I'm lonely and it's no way to live. And so I've let myself love you. God knows why." She laughed, harsh little choppy sounds.

They rode on for a long while, both staring straight ahead, the space between them much wider than the physical gap on the seat.

After a while he asked, "You okay?" "Yes, thank you."

"When will you leave?"

"I don't know yet. I may just ride on out and check on the roundup in a week or two, then go with them from there." She paused, glanced at him. "Will you be going?"

He squeezed the reins so tightly his hands tingled. "I guess not. I may ride on out to Idaho Territory." Going back, back to the way it was before. The long rides into nothingness, accompanied by only painful flashes of memory, never the good times, always the bad. Standing on the edge praying a strong wind would push him off.

He glanced at the woman beside him, chin held so high, so proud, despite the bruises. His heart swelled, his vision narrowed until all he could see was her battered body at the far end of a long, long tunnel. Unreachable. He would ride away and disappear, try to forget her, be no more successful than he had been at forgetting Celia and Fawn. But knowing that would be far better than watching her go to her fate. He could almost see her death, so vivid was the apprehension.

At the gate to the ranch, he turned the team, letting them move along at their own slow pace to prolong the inevitable.

She felt as if her heart were breaking, as if she could hear the cracks and feel the wrenching apart of each blood vessel, of each cell, the living flesh ripped and torn. This couldn't happen, she wouldn't let it.

The ranch house and barn, the bunkhouse and the new cookhouse, grew to life-size before them. This was her home, where she belonged, riding free. She turned and looked at the man beside her, the man she loved. How could he ask her to make such a choice? Whatever happened with the ranch, her father's dream transpired into her own, she must remain who and what she was. Couldn't he see that?

Yet, there was more to life than taking, there was giving, too. It would break her heart, her spirit, if he rode away from her. There must be no more lonely nights. With a sigh she asked, "Would we have children?" She hadn't guessed she would ask that question until it was out.

He hauled up on the reins, dropped them, moved toward her. Relief burst through him like spring sunlight, a joy so supreme he wanted to shout to the heavens. "Oh, Charlie" was all, though, that he could say before enveloping her in his arms, burying his nose in her silken hair. "Yes, yes, we'll have children."

She clung to him, squeezing so tightly it made her arms

ache with the effort. "I won't give up the ranch. Not that. The other, maybe, but not the ranch. We will live here."

"Of course, here. Oh, Charlie, I love you."

He kissed her throat, her jaw, nibbled at her chin and nose, then opened his mouth over hers, drawing in her sweet essence.

When at last they drew a little apart to gaze at one another, it was as if a new day had dawned, separate from all the rest, with promises of its own. Everything would be fresh, all the old scars healed. They believed that, each of them, fervently and absolutely.

She felt a stirring, a dark nameless menace uncoiling from the very depths of her soul, but she pushed it down to bask in the light of their love. Nothing was ever perfect, and she was foolish to expect it to be so. You took the most of the good and the least of the bad and made the best out of it you possibly could. That's what her father always said, and he was right, of course.

With trembling fingers she traced the scar into the white streak of hair. He closed his eyes to memories of the past her touch evoked. Too long he had worn the mark like a symbol of his failure, the emptiness in his life. He captured her hand, pulled it down to his mouth, and sucked at each finger, then traced the lines in her palm with the tip of his tongue.

"You're my love," he murmured into the flesh there, "my life."

She shivered with desire, a wanton sensation that shocked her with its intensity. "Let's go, let's go home," she finally told him shakily.

He nodded and took up the reins. She wrapped her hands through the crook of his arm as they rode into the yard and toward the barn.

Settled cozily in the cabin that no longer seemed so empty, so lonely, they chatted, sitting close together so they could touch. The wedding would not take place until after everyone returned from Cheyenne, they decided. It would be the biggest celebration the territory had ever seen. In their happiness they even agreed to invite the colonel. He would see that they were forming a strong union and stop this ridiculous range war. He would learn they could all live in peace in this vast country.

It was as if speaking of the colonel, even in such an abstract way, somehow brought the man himself to the Double H, for he arrived that very afternoon in a fine black and gold buggy pulled by a spirited red mare. Wolf was with him, doing the driving, and he hopped down and went to the other side to assist the large man down from the single seat.

For a moment she remained in the doorway, then squaring her shoulders, she walked out on the porch, followed by Mitch. For some reason she didn't want the colonel in her home, and hoped to prevent that by speaking with him on the porch. Not very hospitable, but considering the circumstances, she thought it forgivable.

The colonel tilted his head to gaze at her standing at the top of the three steps and removed his hat.

"Miss Houston, I see you are on the mend."

She nodded and that's when Mitch stepped out of the deep shadows under the sloping roof to stand at her side.

The colonel showed little surprise. "Mr. Fallon, I had heard you were a hand over here, but surely they could use you on the roundup, or was the Double H able to hire more hands?"

"What do you want, Dunkirk?" Mitch said, and stepped down so he was standing between the colonel and Charlie.

The colonel held his ground, not at all intimidated. "I came to talk to Miss Houston. Business. In private. If you don't mind."

"As it happens, I do," Mitch said.

"And as it happens, do you have that right?" the colonel asked, smirking.

Charlie stepped out from behind Mitch. "As it happens, Colonel, he does." Mitch had studied this man closely in the several encounters he'd had with him, and never once had he seen him show surprise or doubt. It flickered through his close set eyes now.

"Ah, well I suppose I shouldn't wonder. A fine looking woman like you, all alone to run this—well, this rather shoddy place. It follows that the first smooth-talking good-looking man who comes along could get himself a profitable toehold.

"I should be most careful if I were you, dear lady. Men like Fallon here are experienced at deceit. He will have his hands on all your, uhm—*assets* before you can look twice."

Mitch tensed at her side, the bodyguard Wolf responded in kind, but remained a few steps away in the yard.

"Why, Colonel," she said sweetly before Mitch could react further, "I'm surprised at your concern. All along I thought that was your intent."

Nothing fazed the uniformed man, and he merely smiled and spent some time glancing over the outbuildings, as if he had come to buy. "Not much of a place, is it? But then, it's the land that counts, isn't it? And you have how much?"

"I'm sure you know exactly how much. My father and I each claimed the maximum allowed by law. Of course, we didn't hire anyone to get any illegally for us."

"Ah, but you, like the rest of us, run your cattle on free range, dear lady, technically claiming it as your own."

"What do you want, Dunkirk?" Mitch asked again. "Cut the bull and get to what you came here for."

"Yes, well. I came to make the lady one final offer for the Double H before—well, before—"

"You burn it to the ground? Get out. I don't want to sell, not to you or anyone else. This is my place. My father died for it."

The colonel eyed her savagely for a moment. "And, my dear woman, you may do the same."

Mitch was at the colonel's throat before Wolf could move or Charlie could cry out.

He wrestled the fat man out into the yard and punched viciously at his face. Wolf let out a savage growl and landed on Mitch, hooking a thick arm around his neck from behind and dragging him off the heaving colonel. Mitch was a big man, but Wolf stood two or three inches taller and probably outweighed him by forty or fifty pounds. He pitched Mitch halfway across the yard with seemingly little effort. Mitch skidded and rolled, but amazingly was back on his feet like a supple animal and charged Wolf, who had turned to help the colonel up off the ground.

Mitch's hurtling body hit Wolf low, just as the man pulled the colonel upright.

When he smashed into the huge bodyguard, all three went down into a pile that for a moment looked all arms and legs and one large belly.

Charlie waited no longer, but ran inside to fetch her Winchester from the corner, jacked a round into the chamber, and hurried back outside. By the time she stumbled down the steps into the yard, the colonel sat dazed and bewildered while Mitch beat Wolf bloody. The man had already stopped fighting back, but Mitch kept pounding him, pulling him within reach, hitting him, and when he staggered as if to fall, propping him upright for another round.

For a moment she stared, transfixed by such sheer brutality. She had expected to come back out here to save Mitch's hide. God knew, she wouldn't have shot anyone, or at least she didn't think she would have. Now what did she do? Wait till Mitch beat the man to a bloody pulp, or make the gesture anyway and put a stop to this ridiculous situation.

The decision was easily made, for she hated watching anyone get beaten so badly.

She pointed the gun on a slant into the air and fired off a shot, jacked another round into the chamber and fired it, too. Mitch hunched his shoulders, hesitated for a moment without looking back at her, and Wolf fell, first to his knees, then flat on his face. With a roar Mitch bent down, grabbed the unconscious man by the collar of his shirt and the back of his belt to drag him over to the colonel, who had finally managed to stagger to his feet.

"Take your filth out of here before I kill him," Mitch said through gasps. "You stay away from here and from her." He whirled and pointed at Charlie where she stood holding the Winchester down at her side. "Or I'll let her shoot you, you son of a bitch."

Her mouth dropped open. As amazed as she'd been at the fury Mitch had displayed, at his obvious intent to actually beat the man Wolf to death, she was even more amazed that he could say such a thing in an almost humorous tone.

The colonel retrieved his hat from where it had fallen in the grass and sparing only one glance for his bloody bodyguard huffed out to the buggy and climbed aboard.

With disdain he spat in the dust, then said, "I'll send someone for him. If you decide to kill him, let me know and I won't waste my time. I've got more where he came from. More than you can imagine. If you're smart you'll take what you can get for your shipment of beeves and light out, because nothing is going to stop me from having all the land. Certainly not one burnt-out gunslinger and a female who can't shoot straight."

Four

For several moments Charlie gaped after the colonel's buggy and the thin trail of dust it left.

"I ought to show you how straight I can shoot, you old fool," she shouted into the wind, but didn't raise the gun, for she had remembered Mitch.

He stood staring down at the unconscious Wolf, and she went to him. "Are you hurt?" She pulled him around to inspect his face. Other than a trickle of blood from a small cut on one cheekbone he didn't have a mark on him. She put an arm around his waist and he squeezed her shoulder, grimaced.

"1 think I broke my damned hand," he said.

"Come on inside, I'll clean it up, we'll see. It wouldn't be any wonder. I thought you were going to beat him to death."

Mitch shrugged. "He was going to do the same to me. I just did it first, that's all."

She glanced nervously up at him. The violence he'd unleashed was an awesome thing, and she wasn't sure she liked it. This man kept a lot more hidden than she would ever have guessed.

"What shall we do with him?" She gestured toward Wolf, who showed no signs of coming to.

Mitch touched him with the toe of his boot. "Poor bastard." "Poor?"

"He did what he was paid to do and that no-good Dunkirk just leaves him lying here like a discarded carcass."

She grinned.

"What the hell is so funny?" he asked, and began to inspect his swollen, battered knuckles.

"You are. You beat the man senseless, then feel sorry for him. I don't know what I was worried about."

They went up the steps together and crossed the porch into the house without speaking. Inside, she made him sit in a chair while she immersed his hands in a pan of cold water to take down the swelling.

He concentrated on her ministrations for a while, then asked, "What did you mean, you didn't know what you were worried about?"

"Oh, nothing really." "Yes, you did. Tell me."

"I was—well, a little unnerved when you... when you wouldn't stop hitting that man. It was so violent, so brutal, and I guess I'd never actually seen that side of you before."

He nodded, waited while she tore strips of cotton feed sack to bind his right fist. Tongue between her lips she gently wrapped the battered hand and tied off the bandage.

"I'm sorry if I scared you," he said when she'd finished. "Well, you did."

"But then?" "Then what?"

"You said you didn't know—"

"Oh, yes. That. When I saw the pity in your eyes and you actually felt sorry for your victim, well, I guess I realized I had nothing to worry about."

He circled her neck with his left hand, the one that had only delivered a few blows and hadn't suffered drastically from the fight, and pulled her toward him. "The only thing you've got to worry about, darlin', is feeding me before I starve to death."

Her eyes grew wide, her mouth pursed. "Oh, dear."

"What?" he asked softly. He leaned close, kissed her lightly under one ear. "Well, I can't...." She shivered as he nibbled down the side of her neck. "Go on," he said and took a big love bite.

"I forgot to tell you, I can't...."

He pulled the collar of the dress down as far as he could, fiddled with the buttons at her throat, and kissed her in the deep vee between her breasts. his hot breath making her tremble. "Can't?"

"Cook," she blurted. "I can't *cook*. Oh, dear, Mitch."

She collapsed into his arms, while he worked the dress open with one hand, slowly, awkwardly. His mouth followed the parting of material with such leisurely passion that Charlie gathered handfuls of his shirt and yanked, trying to make him move faster.

He stopped abruptly. Hot breath in and out, moistening the skin where his mouth waited.

"What? What is it?" she asked, almost frantic with desire.

"You can't cook? You can't *cook*? My God, what am I possibly thinking?"

With that he abandoned breaking trail between her breasts and lifted her into his arms. He carried her to the bed. "Well, that does it, woman. I can't make love to you if you can't cook." He lay her on the mattress very carefully and stood over her, looking down, shaking his head woefully. "Too bad, too. You're a fine-looking woman, even if you do dress kind of funny."

He turned from her, fetched his hat, put it on, and went out the door. She lay there for a moment, not sure whether to take him seriously or not. She waited for him to return, hands lying across her quivering stomach.

After a minute she called, "Mitch?" No answer.

Surely he'd been teasing. Was just lying in wait for her outside the door. "Mitch, where are you?"

He stuck his head around the doorjamb. "Ma'am, I was just thinking maybe I'd better pour a bucket of water over this poor fellow. I'd hate for him to lay out here and die while we're having all this fun. Wait right where you are, don't move. I have a feeling we're going to have to discuss this cooking thing." He pointed a finger at her, grinned, and bounded off the porch.

In a little while she crawled carefully off the bed, still favoring her sore muscles, and went to the door. Mitch had revived Wolf and both were sitting in the yard side by side deep in a very serious conversation. Quietly she closed the door and took off the dress, stripping right down to the buff, immensely relieved to be rid of the long stockings and hateful lace-up shoes. Then she pulled on her BVDs, jeans and chambray shirt, thick white socks and a pair of boots, not the ones she'd worn on roundup, for she couldn't find them anywhere.

Then she went out to sit on the porch. Wolf and Mitch were nowhere to be seen, but she wasn't worried. It wasn't long before Wolf rode out of the barn on a mustang, one of hers no doubt, and Mitch came walking across the yard. She rose to go meet him, and when he saw her in her range-riding clothes, he raised an eyebrow but said nothing.

"Still hungry?" she asked. "A lot of good it'll do me."

"I've got some canned peaches."

"Well, I suppose I can live on canned peaches... and love."
"Do you think so?"

He stopped right there in the middle of the yard and pulled her close. "I know so."

Someone rode up in the yard in a big hurry, shouting for Charlie, for anyone, in a loud frantic voice.

It was Ritter.

Heart in her throat Charlie turned to face the man.

"Oh, Gawd, Miss Charlie. Thank God you're here. And

Fallon, too." He stopped to get his breath. Under him, the horse danced and snorted.

"What? Ritter, what in the world—?"

"It's Mr. Yancey. They've killed him. Blasted sons a bitches have killed him. And P.J., he lit into one of 'em and got his arm broke for his troubles." Ritter stopped again, dismounting from the excited horse. It ran off toward the corral whinnying.

"Who? For God's sake, Yancey dead?" She stared through tears. Mitch put an arm around her shoulder. "Who did this, Ritter? *Tell* me!"

"One of them blamed gunsels of the colonel's. Rode up on us out of nowhere.

Started in on Yancey, you know how he was. Couldn't rile him if you tried. Knew better than to outright shoot him, so they just kept picking and picking. Finally set him off and he went for his rifle. Never got it out of the scabbard. Just shot him. Dang it, it was murder, pure and simple."

She staggered into Mitch's grasp. Not Yancey. Not dear, sweet Yancey. "I knew him all my life," she cried into Mitch's chest, the world swirling blackly around her.

"Are you sure he's dead?" Mitch asked Ritter, holding on to her tightly. "Wasn't when I left, but they shot him right through the chest with a .44. Ain't nothin' would save a man from that."

She grabbed Mitch's shoulders. "We've got to go to him, now, before it's too late."

He nodded, a black dread rising in his throat. He wished he could take her far away to some safe place where nothing could ever harm her, where no one could get close enough to bring her pain. But he knew that would never happen, because there wasn't any such place. Not for this woman, and certainly not for him.

Despite Mitch's objections, Charlie insisted on riding

out to see about Yancey. "Just let me hitch up the buckboard at least," he pleaded, even as he saddled a mean-tempered buckskin for her. The choice horses were all in the remuda with the roundup.

"You know I can do that myself. And I can ride. I'm only sore, not broke."

Mitch yanked the latigo through the cinch. The buckskin grunted and kicked out.

"Dang knothead. Charlie, dammit, you've got no business riding this half-broke mustang."

She shooed him away and stepped her left toe into the stirrup. "You just take care of yourself, Mitchell Fallon, and I'll do the same." Swinging deftly into the saddle, she hauled back on the reins just hard enough to let the horse know who was boss. "Settle down before I take a board to you," she said, then scratched the fractious horse behind one ear.

The mustang darted sideways and tossed his head trying to dislodge the bit. She kicked him into a gallop, leaving Mitch and Ritter staring after her. The half-wild buckskin wasn't Belle, nor did he give the smooth easy ride of the poor little lost roan, but she rode him wildly and at full tilt out across the field, turned, and rode back into the yard. The ride set all her muscles to aching and she was reminded of her near miss under the stampeding cattle.

She smiled grimly down on the two men. "He's fine, he'll do. You coming or not?" Dusk closed around the trio as they reached camp, and every muscle and bone in Charlie's body cried out for relief. She tried to hide her pain from Mitch, but he guessed and insisted on helping her down off the mustang. That she allowed such a thing told him all he needed to know, but he didn't try to stop her when she broke into a run on spying Yancey lying beside the fire.

P.J. spoke first and loudest when she sank to her knees beside her beloved ramrod. "I tried to stop 'em, Miss Charlie. But they just flat out shot him. Throwed me off my horse and busted my arm." He cradled the arm close to his body, staring into the fire because he couldn't bear to look at her.

"He's still breathing," she said softly. She laid a hand on Yancey's forehead and his eyelids flickered.

The sound he made wasn't exactly a word, though it apparently was intended to be.

"Hush, now. You'll be fine." She looked up and around at the men, some of whom had just wandered over. Most of course were out gathering cattle. "Has anyone sent for the doctor?"

"We did that, Miss Charlie. Soon as it happened."

"Crane done what he could, too," another added.

"And the doc, he ain't in town. Trent come back just a while ago and said he had gone to a place up on the Missouri. Some feller fell out of his loft and broke his back. A nester."

She turned back the blanket to inspect the hole in Yancey's chest. His shirt had been ripped away and a crude dressing applied to the wound. It was soaked with blood. She removed the cloth with a grimace. The blue-black hole, about the size of her middle finger, oozed blood.

"Did the bullet go clean through?"

Crane appeared from the cluster of men. "A .44 Winchester, at close range.

Must've missed every bone he's got in there. It come out the back all right. Left him an even bigger hole. I covered it up best I could. You know chest wounds, Miss Houston. If he's lung shot, well, then we can just wait for him to die."

"Or not," she shouted at the man. "He can hear you."

The cook shrugged as if it made no difference, then dissolved back into the small gathering of men.

She found Yancey's clammy, feverish hand and held it in both hers. "Now you listen to me, Yancey Barton. You will not die and leave me with all this. Not after all we've been through together."

Yancey moved his lips into a grin that looked more like a grimace of pain. "Couldn't—couldn't face old Matt—if I did that," he gasped out. "And I'm sure headed the same place." What might have passed for a chuckle turned into a groan and the man fell silent.

"Well, you're just not going to die. I won't let you. Crane, get me some hot water and clean rags and something for bandages."

She had Mitch turn Yancey gently so she could wash and bandage the wound in his back, then carefully folded a clean blanket and lay it on the bloodied one before easing the groaning man down. Mitch held the washpan close so she could clean the chest wound, then tore strips from the cotton fabric to tie the bandage on.

After giving Yancey some more whiskey to help him sleep, Mitch and Charlie found bedding of their own for the night.

"I wish you didn't have to sleep out on the ground so soon after our accident," Mitch told her when she lowered herself very carefully. "I'm going to go rustle us up some supper. Crane's got a pot on the fire. Whatever's in it'll beat what we've had so far today."

"Mitch?" She looked up at him gratefully. He turned, waited.

"Thank you."

Jaw clenched, he nodded. Damndest most stubborn woman he'd ever met in his life. As he looked down into her glistening dark eyes, a fist took hold of his heart and squeezed until he gasped. How he loved her. Dear God, if anything happened to her he couldn't live, and he'd probably be so insane with grief he'd take half the world with him when he went.

Fetching food for the two of them had only been half the

reason Mitch left Charlie's side. Within him had swelled a bitter hatred, a need for revenge against the men who had struck once more at the woman he loved. He wanted to ask some questions out of her hearing. He signaled P.J. to follow him away from the campfire, and the young cowboy did so, despite the obvious pain of the broken arm.

Together they stood near the chuck wagon.

"Who were those men that shot your ramrod?"

P.J. frowned. "Two of those gunslingers the colonel hired. I don't know names." "Then tell me what they looked like."

"One was big and ugly, wore a right fancy silver buckle and leather holster. The other was a fat little runt, looked like a damned kid not dry behind the ears. He kept giggling like his wheelbarrow wasn't fully loaded. Might not have been, but he could use a gun just the same.

"Mister, I did my best to stop what happened. I even took a shot at them after they knocked me off my horse. It was no use. Hell, I'd fight for Miss Charlie, but I ain't no gunslinger, I'm a dang cowboy."

Mitch patted the man on his uninjured shoulder.

"Hey, I know. You did all you could. It's that Cross and Neddy that's to blame for this, not you."

P.J. pointed at him. "Yeah, that's it. That tubby feller called the other'n Cross, and I forgot till you said it. Cross, that's it. The ugly one's name was Cross."

Mitch nodded. "I'll be riding out later tonight, after everyone is asleep." He glanced quickly toward Charlie, who sat near Yancey staring into the fire. "I don't come back, you see Ritter takes care of her, you hear?"

"I'll watch her myself, too," P.J. declared. "She's a plumb brave woman, good as any man I ever saw."

"You do that, but tell Ritter to keep an eye on her till I get back, and not let her do anything too foolish. And tell him to be careful of Crane, you understand?"

"The cook?"

Mitch nodded, picked up two tin plates, and began to fill them both with beans from the kettle hanging over the dying fire. "Just tell him, he'll know what to do, take my word for it."

Carrying the steaming plates of beans seasoned with fatback and two Johnny cakes, Mitch tried to envision the life he and Charlie would have together, the happiness they would find, the children they would bring into this vast Montana Territory once this mess with the colonel was cleared up. The kids would be stubborn and pretty like her, mean and strong like him. They'd whip the world, they would.

"What're you grinning at?" Charlie asked as she took the plate.

"I was just thinking of our kids. What they'll look like with you and me for folks." "Oh, Mitch." She wiped her eyes on the back of her hand.

"Hey, he's going to be fine. Eat up. You need to get your strength back if you intend to keep on traipsing around, and I reckon you do."

They both cleaned their plates before retiring side by side. He held her in his arms until her breathing evened out, little puffs of air flowing over his face tucked down against hers. Then he eased carefully from the embrace, dug his six-shooter from his pack and went to saddle the stallion.

At his approach the black nickered and pulled at the rope tying him to the corral. Horses around him whinnied and trampled the ground, but quieted after Mitch led his mount away. He waited until he was out of view of the camp before he mounted up and rode toward the Circle D and a showdown with Cross and Neddy. It had been a long time coming.

When Mitch hadn't returned by the time the doc arrived

at camp the next day, Charlie, as Ritter put it, "had a wall-eyed fit." He thought for a while he was going to have to tie her up to keep her there. If it hadn't been for Yancey, she would have ridden out in search of Fallon. As it was, she chose to ride with the wounded ramrod back to Miles City in the back of Doc's wagon. She was afraid he wouldn't live, and she refused to let him die alone with no one holding his hand.

She couldn't find Mitch anywhere in Miles City, but didn't have much of a clue as to where to look. She did, however, catch up on news about the Indian troubles. After General Terry pulled the fat out of the fire, saving Reno and Benteen who had ridden in on the heels of Custer's defeat, the tide of battle had shifted. The army had the Indians on the run. She grieved for all those who had died on both sides and most especially the innocent victims. But there was nothing she could do and she had Yancey and Mitch to worry about.

As the days passed without word from Mitch, her heart turned to ice. Despite all his words, he had left her. It was obvious. On the fourth day of Yancey's confinement, when he began to show some real sign that he truly would recover, she rode out early and headed for the Circle D Ranch. If anyone there had seen Mitchell Fallon they probably wouldn't tell her, but she had no place else to look.

When the colonel greeted her before she could dismount she didn't know what to say. He was responsible for so much heartache that what she wanted to do was yank her Winchester from its scabbard and shoot him between the eyes. Instead, she held her fury in check and played the game by his rules.

"Why, what a pleasant surprise, Miss Houston. You honor me. Light awhile. Would you like a cold drink?"

She licked at dry lips, removed her hat, and blotted sweat from her forehead with the curve of her arm. Much as it galled her to accept refreshment from the man, she couldn't resist, and swung down from the horse.

"That would be nice, thank you." Her tone was scarcely civil.

They sat on the porch, the colonel looking well pleased. "Now, tell me, what brings you out to the back forty on such a day? Are we ready to make a deal?"

She played with her hat a moment, then put it on the floor beside her, tented her fingers, and, without looking at the colonel for fear of what she might see there, remarked as casually as she could, "I wonder if you've seen Mitchell Fallon lately?"

The colonel threw back his head and laughed. Before she could react, a man she had never seen before came out carrying a tray with a pitcher and two glasses. He wore guns on both hips, and she couldn't help but think about how silly he looked serving them drinks, as if he were a maid.

After the awkward gunman poured them each a glass of cold lemonade, the colonel lifted his as if making a silent toast, then took a sip. She stared at him.

"I could have warned you the man wasn't trustworthy. So now he's left you in the lurch as well. That's too bad. Well, of course, he does still owe me some time. Some men, my dear, realize who the winner will be and that's the side they wish to fight on. Mr. Fallon is one such man, I can assure you."

Heat flushed up her throat and her head throbbed. She drank thirstily from the glass, then thunked it back in the tray and stood up.

"You, sir, are not going to get away with what you're trying to do to all of us. I promise you that. We will stop you. You should never have sent your men after my ramrod, because frankly, Colonel, I don't care much what I have to do to bring you down now.

"My father worked for one of the biggest and best cattlemen Texas ever produced, and he never did the things you have done to earn his fortune. My father, sir, would have spit in your eye and cut you off at the knees, and that is exactly what I will do, sooner or later. You can count on it.

"And if you do see Mr. Fallon, tell him for me that it goes double for him should he choose to stand against me."

The colonel simply opened his arms wide as if to say, here I am, do what you will, and then he smiled.

She scooped up her hat, hitting the edge of the table so that the pitcher and glasses rattled. One toppled to the floor, shattering in hundreds of glistening pieces that crunched under her boots as she strode across the porch.

Weary and sad, she rode on over to the Double H, expecting to find no one there. An extra horse browsed in the corral with the few unbroken mustangs. She turned her buckskin in with them, planning on staying overnight before riding back to see about Yancey.

Carrying the Winchester, she went up to the house to see who was there. The sun hung on the lip of the mountains far to the west and the air had begun to cool. She wanted a bath and a long night's sleep in her own bed. Instead she would have to deal with a visitor. A drift of smoke came from the fireplace chimney at the cabin. Someone had settled into the place, a drifter perhaps, or maybe even a squatter who thought the place abandoned.

She jacked a shell into the breech and crept quietly up the steps, staying to one side of the door.

"Whoever's in there, come on out, hands where I can see them." She lifted the rifle to her waist.

The door creaked slowly open and Wolf filled the doorway. He held both hands out away from his hips, but he wore no gun.

His pockmarked, lupine face lit with what passed for a grin. "Sorry, ma'am. I worried about the place. Decided to look after it. I'll get my stuff, get out of your way."

She grinned a little herself and sighed with relief, lowering her rifle barrel so it pointed at the porch floor.

The man showed no signs of the beating Mitch had given him, even the worst of the cuts and bruises had plenty of time to heal. She insisted he stay, and he moved his stuff to the bunkhouse with what appeared to be pleasure. With Wolf it was difficult to tell.

"I'm afraid I can't offer you supper," she said from the doorway of the bunkhouse. "I'm only going to be here overnight."

She watched the man arrange his things beside the bunk, and then he looked up shyly. "I been here since, well, since the fight. Didn't have a place to go. I hope—I mean, I'll leave."

"Nonsense. I'm shorthanded. The colonel surely won't welcome you with open arms."

"They come to burn you out. I run them off." "My God," she said. "When? I mean, thank you."

He nodded and sat on the bunk, his long legs splayed. After a moment's silence, he looked at her as if to say, what next?

"Have you seen Mitchell Fallon?" she asked, misery and shame in her voice. She hated what his leaving had done to her. How long could she chase around after this man who obviously wanted nothing more to do with her.

"He the one?" Wolf ran a curved thumb above his own eyelid into the hairline. "Yes, him."

"Did they get him, you reckon?"

The possibility hadn't occurred to her, and she flinched as if struck. "My God, do you think so? I mean, I never thought, he is—well, so capable. He's survived so much. He talked once about riding on to Idaho, but dear God, you don't suppose?"

Wolf unwrapped his legs and arms and stood, the top of his head almost touching the low-hung log rafters. "Hey, no, you're probably right. The way he handled himself." He wryly fingered his own jaw. "And I know for a fact no one could take him in a gunfight. The man was fast and mean as a snake when he wanted to be."

Feeling some measure of relief she nodded. She couldn't decide which would be worse, Mitch leaving her or Mitch shot down by some other hard case. She didn't want him dead, no matter what he decided to do.

They had no more to say to each other, so she told him to stay as long as he liked, added that she would appreciate it and would see he was compensated come payday.

"I think I'll just go to Cheyenne with the herd," she said over her shoulder. "Make yourself at home." She took her leave then, and trudged to the empty cabin.

Five

Charlie, Ritter, and Crane returned from Cheyenne in early October to find Wolf and Yancey Barton at the ranch. Yancey was stove up some, but on the way to a full recovery. Every time he had to sit and rest a spell he would nearly foam at the mouth with impatience. Neither he nor Wolf had seen hide nor hair of Mitch Fallon, but it was common knowledge that he had gunned down both Cross and Neddy in a gunfight and then disappeared. Word was that the sheriff, under the colonel's prodding, was looking for him for murder.

With a heavy heart, Charlie settled down to the business of readying the ranch for the coming winter. While happy to learn that Mitch hadn't left her deliberately, she could hardly bear the thought of him being hunted like some wild animal, and hoped that he had indeed ridden off to Idaho Territory.

As for the range war, the shooting of Cross and Neddy seemed to have taken some of the wind out of the colonel's sails. No one expected that to last long. Now that everyone was back from roundup, he would, as promised, get serious. The colonel had ordered the ranchers to take their profits and leave the territory. A few did, but most swore to stay and fight. So the next round was sure to begin, and soon.

With the prospect of another lonely winter stretching

ahead of her, Charlie missed Mitch dreadfully, but she was fully prepared to do her part in holding off the colonel and his men.

Radine spotted Duffy McGrew in the crowd at the Powder Keg. Word was his wife had left him and gone back to Denver to be with her parents. The Stallings had bankrolled the ranch, everyone knew that, and Duffy was furious and drinking heavily.

As she delivered a round of beers, she overheard something that made her fear for her friend Charlie Houston.

"That son of a bitch Fallon ain't nothing but a no-good Yank," McGrew said to his cronies gathered around the table. "Give me half a chance I'd shoot that cowardly no-good. I know things about him he wouldn't want told."

Bending across the table, Radine deliberately let her full breasts lie on McGrew's arm. She wanted to learn more, and knew only one way to do it.

The rancher peered down the front of her scanty chemise, then stuck a folded bill there.

"Come on, baby," Radine said and took his hand.

The already staggering McGrew followed her upstairs.

Her only fear was that he would pass out before she could worm the information she wanted from him. But it was easier than she had thought, for he obviously needed to talk to someone and all she had to do was bring up the gunslinger's name.

"Damn traitor," McGrew said. "I was with him in the war and woulda followed him anywhere and did. We had a gang and was doing just fine till his sister led the vigilantes to our hideout." He paused and fumbled at her naked breasts. "Pretty things. My wife don't like me to touch her there."

Radine smiled seductively. "What did he do?"

"Left us. Run out when the dang sheriff and his band of killers showed up. Most of us was killed, but not me—no, sir. And I know where there's others, too.

"Oh, honey, come closer and let old Duffy have some of that." "I will, baby. I will."

She snuggled up against the man, who was so drunk he couldn't perform, but he could talk.

"Kill him, hang him up in some tree for the buzzards. Teach him to run out on us, leave us for the wolves. Everyone can come spit on the sumbitch. Sent my man for the marshal, but he never come back. Neither one of 'em. Injuns probably got him."

"The marshal?"

McGrew snorted, but didn't reply. "Jest wait, you'll see."

He took a deep rattling breath and his head lolled away from her. She slipped from the loose embrace of the snoring, drunken McGrew, sat on the edge of the bed, and slipped into her robe. She was worried about the things he'd said. Worried for that handsome devil with the white streak in his hair and her friend Charlie Houston. The two of them had been mighty cozy, and then that awful gunfight. Radine had visited with Charlie a few times while she was laid up after her accident, but hadn't seen her since all the ranchers had ridden back from Cheyenne. She wondered if it would be considered proper for her to ride out for a visit before the winter storms cut them all off from one another. Good women friends were hard to find for someone like her.

Thinking of all the man on her bed had said, Radine decided she didn't care if it was proper or not. Charlie needed to know what she'd heard. First thing in the morning she would borrow Lance's buggy and ride out. She hated horses and never rode one.

She had other uses for those particular parts of her body than getting them chafed raw by a leather saddle and the plodding of some dumb animal.

"This is really nice," Radine remarked when Charlie enthusiastically welcomed her into her home the next morning.

The neat and cozy little cabin sure beat the dump she lived in, and she thought what it might be like to have something like this.

"It's okay for one person. We had plans for a bigger place, my father and I, but then he was killed before—well, before we got here." Charlie swallowed hard over the words, then smiled. "I never expected you, but it's wonderful to have a visitor. I'll make us some tea."

Radine nodded and sat where Charlie indicated, one of two straight-backed chairs at a small square table in one corner of the single room. A bed was shoved against another wall, and a stove used both for cooking and supplementing the heat of the fireplace sat across from the front door.

Charlie pulled a kettle onto the stove where a small fire crackled. The nights had grown chilly and she'd built a fire every morning since returning from Cheyenne. Winter would soon be upon them.

"Would you like some music? I have a music box. Let me get it." Charlie started toward the bed.

"I came to tell you something. Music would be nice. Maybe later. This is important."

Charlie twisted around at the serious tone in Radine's voice. Her cherub face carried a frown that took away its usual gaiety. She forgot the music box and went to sit in the chair near Radine.

"What is it? You look so... so intense."

Radine nodded and fiddled with the hem of her best shawl worn specially for this occasion. She did not go calling often and felt unsure of herself. "It's about...about that man, the tall man with the white streak in his hair?"

Charlie's heart tumbled around until she had to catch her breath. "What about him? Tell me, have you seen him? Is he all right? Is it true what they say about him being wanted for murder? Oh, Radine, please."

"I remembered how you felt about him, that's why I came all the way out here. I thought you might get a message to him. If he's still around he needs to light out. Go far and fast."

Charlie nodded. "But I'm sure he knows that. He must know the sheriff is looking for him."

"Oh, no, it's worse than that. The sheriff is the least of his troubles. That old fart couldn't scare anyone with both guns drawing a bead. He can't see across the street. No, this is someone else. Someone who'll do a lot worse than arrest him for murder."

"What are you talking about?" Charlie felt as if her life were seeping out of her through tiny holes, and she would never get it back.

"That McGrew fella, owns the ranch up north near the Missouri?" Charlie nodded, waited.

Radine told her what Duffy McGrew had said as their tea grew cold in its cups. By the time she was finished Radine was practically in tears.

Charlie gaped at her. The only sound in the room was the sizzling of water in the kettle until she dragged in a deep breath. "My God. Is everyone in the world crazy? Did he say...does he have any idea where Mitch is? I mean, I haven't seen him. He could be anywhere. That's probably it. Mitch is probably not even around here anymore. He's gone, I'm sure. Long gone where no one can find him."

She clasped Radine's fisted hands in hers and gazed into her wide eyes, a racking pain shooting through her chest.

Outside the wind kicked up, rattling the golden leaves in the aspen trees along the ridge behind the house, and on the stove the water continued to boil, untended.

❁

Mitch led the black through the falling shadows of night, pausing a moment before venturing into the open between the draw and Charlie's cabin. A cold wind cut through his shirt, and he wished again for a good thick mackinaw.

She was in there, he could see a glow through the deer hides tacked over the windows to keep out the cold night air. He didn't dare approach for fear someone was watching the house.

Shivering, he leaned against the warmth of the stallion's quivering shoulder. He should have left the territory days ago, weeks ago, even before he'd hunted down that devil Cross and his crazy sidekick Neddy. Now he didn't know how he was going to protect her against what was sure to come. If he revealed himself anyone could shoot him and get away with it. Colonel Dunkirk and the sheriff had seen to that with the bounty they'd put on his head for murder. It would be paid for his dead body, no questions asked.

A clattering sound caught his attention and he raised his head into the wind.

Something furtive had rattled through gravel. A man? An animal? He listened, checked the stallion for signs he'd heard it, but the horse remained docile, too weary to act up. He just stood hipshot, hindquarters turned to the wind, head down.

"I think both of us sort of feel the same way, old buddy," Mitch whispered.

Bits of icy moisture struck his cheeks and the brisk smell of high country snow rode on the wind. He pawed around in his saddlebags, dragged out a blanket and canvas poncho. He wrapped up in both and settled down to keep an eye on the cabin. Soon the airborne pellets turned to flakes. The first snow of the season and him without home or hearth. The light in the cabin, her invisible presence nearby, tugged at him, and he wanted only to hold her in his arms while they lay together near a warm fire.

Did he dare? No one would see him, surely. There were no lights in the bunkhouse, and she would probably have let all the men go except Ritter and Yancey and that sneaky Crane. He'd been on the verge of figuring out what to do about the traitorous man and his obvious connection to Dunkirk when Yancey was shot.

A shadow flitted across the window shade at the back of the house and he hunched deeper into the shadows. The back door cracked open, letting out a thin ribbon of light. Then she was standing there, door thrown open. She stepped out into the blowing snow, leaving the door wide so that he could see her plainly. He gasped with the beauty of her shapely long legs, supple curves to a narrow waist, and uptilted breasts hugged by the gossamer windblown gown.

Dear God, how he wanted to hold her, smell her, feel the silkiness of her skin.

He stepped out into the open, called her name softly, realized that she couldn't hear him for the wind, and called out again.

She stood in the snow for a moment, face tilted upward so that flakes caught at her eyelashes and melted on her cheeks. Riding the wind her name echoed like a vaguely recalled dream, and she opened her eyes, peered into the blowing snow.

"Mitch? Where are you?" She didn't expect a reply except in her wishful imagination.

Out of the darkness and wall of hurtling flakes appeared a shadowy figure, and again her name repeated. "Charlie. Charlie."

It was clear and real this time.

Joy exploded through her like sunlight on a spring day. It was Mitch. Ignoring bare feet and the frozen ground, she started to run, and at that precise moment a rifle shot rent the storm-swept night. A horse screamed and the shadow pitched forward without making a sound.

She shrieked and ran to the fallen man, oblivious to the prickly shrubs and rocks and tough sprigs of dried grass that chewed at her feet. She ignored the frigid wind and the icy pellets, felt only the searing pain in her heart. Kneeling beside him, she brushed a fan of snow-crusted hair from the side of his face and leaned close.

"Mitch? Oh, Mitch."

He moaned, tried to move. "Charlie?"

"Yes, oh, yes. Darling. We've got to get you inside."

He moved one arm, raised himself on that side. "Horse, get my horse."

She glanced around. It was so dark, she could see nothing but what was illuminated by the light coming from her open doorway. "I don't see—"

"There, back there. Call—call him."

That turned out not to be necessary. The stallion emerged out of the darkness, nosing his master and snorting.

She reached for the reins, but the black tossed his head high and danced backward.

"Ho," Mitch said raggedly. "Ho down, there."

She darted out a hand, grabbed one dangling rein, and led the nervous animal to Mitch's side.

"Put my arm in the stirrup. Help me."

She could barely make out the weak plea, hurriedly positioned herself under him, and hoisted him up until his crooked elbow threaded through the stirrup. Then she led the horse slowly to the back door, dragging Mitch along. His arm slipped out once and they had to do it all over again. The stallion, skittish at first, finally seemed to understand what was expected of him, and he dragged his master literally to the door. Mitch was unconscious, the upper half of his body sprawled inside, the rest hanging out onto the ground.

Leaning against the huge stallion, she shoved him out of the way, then went inside and began the task of dragging Mitch the rest of the way into the house. It was as tough as wrestling with a thousand-pound steer, but all she could think of was getting him into the warmth. He couldn't die, she wouldn't let him. By the time she had sweated and grunted and strained to lug him inside, she was covered with perspiration and the warmth of the cabin had been replaced by a bone-chilling cold.

She slammed the door, filled the stove and fireplace with wood, then quickly dragged the heavy quilt off the bed. Kneeling beside Mitch she wiped his face gently with both palms. Hot tears of anguish poured down her cheeks. He was pale, tinged blue, and so cold.

Lips covering his, she breathed into his mouth as if she could give him some of her warmth. He made a small, weak sound down in his throat and shuddered.

Quickly she removed his shirt and boots. The blanket and poncho he'd had around him had fallen off in the effort to get him to the house, and she bundled the quilt around him tightly. Getting him warm had to come first, even before seeing to the wound, which wasn't bleeding profusely.

The small room heated up fast, the snow caught in his hair melted and formed a tiny puddle on the plank floor. Her own bare feet began to ache, but she ignored the pain to huddle over him, rubbing his hands briskly. Some color returned to his cheeks but he made no sound. He was breathing, though shallowly.

With trembling fingers she traced his features. The high, rugged brow, the eyes, sunken now, the wide cheekbones and square jawline, the fine nose and full, firm mouth. She touched the jagged scar that ran up into his dark hair and fragments of the pain he had endured shot through her fingertips straight to her soul.

"Oh, Mitch, don't you die. Don't you dare die. Where have you been, my darling?

Where?"

She kissed him softly, then rose and poured boiling water into the washpan, fetched soap and a cloth, and sat down beside him on the floor to clean the wound. She prayed the bullet had gone all the way through, for she had no idea how to dig it out, even if she dared try.

The bullet had caught him high in the right shoulder and torn an ugly hole in the fleshy muscle where it came out. It was bleeding front and back, but not spurting. At least he wouldn't bleed to death. He remained unconscious all the time it took her to clean the two wounds and wrap them tightly. She was relieved because she had no whiskey to give him for the pain.

When she finished she put more wood in both fires, slipped hurriedly into her clothes, and went to take care of his horse. Only then did she begin to wonder who had been skulking around close enough to have seen Mitch in the darkness and shot him.

By the time she returned from the barn, a full-fledged blizzard blew flat across the land, snow so thick she could hardly see the light from the cabin. No telling when it would stop. Maybe a piece of luck for Mitch, maybe not. No one could get to them for a while, and that would give him time to mend before facing the law, but should he need a doctor that could be bad.

Back inside, she found him just as she'd left him.

Kneeling there, she skinned out of her clothes, except for the thick socks and underwear, and crawled under the quilt on the floor beside him. Snuggled close to the man she loved, she soon fell into an exhausted sleep, his heart beating firmly against her cheek.

Sometime before dawn he cried out and tried to roll over. She caught him about the waist with one arm.

"Shh, it's all right, you're okay."

"Charlie, is that you?"

"Yes, darling," she said. "What happened?"

"Shh, be quiet. Go back to sleep." She kissed him, eased him back down. "We'll talk in the morning. You need to rest."

He was quiet for a while, breathing harshly. "Charlie?" "Yes?"

"Are you sure it's you?" "Oh, yes, it's me."

"I'm not dead?"

"No, you're not dead. Now go back to sleep."

He nodded, wrapped his good arm around her shoulders, and pulled her so close she could scarcely breathe. "Okay, I will. That's what I'll...."

She lay very still, ear pressed against his chest, but he had no more to say. For a long while she listened to the wind moaning around the eaves of the little cabin, then she, too, dropped off to sleep.

Mitch opened his eyes and found himself looking at log beams. He hunched, in preparation for climbing to his feet, but an intense pain slammed him flat before he could much more than wiggle.

"What? Where—" He remembered nothing, his mind empty and black as a cave. With a great deal of care against the fire raging in his right shoulder, he rolled his head to one side. Saw the legs of chairs and a table. Carefully he turned the other way to gaze at the bedstead and one side of a potbellied stove. He tried to lick his lips, but found his tongue so dry it clung to the top of his mouth.

What in the hell had happened to him? He couldn't even remember what he was doing last…night? morning? whatever. Nothing made sense.

Someone clattered across the floor, stomping hard with huge boots. A giant.

His head hammered. "Could you—could you quiet down?" he thought he said, but his ears told him different. It was more like gurgle, cough, grunt, gurgle.

She came into view then, kneeling beside him, her face flushed from the cold, her eyes bright and shiny as berries, her fingers touching him. The tips made cold little dots on his cheek.

"Charlie?" he croaked. He would have sung the name if he could have managed. "Oh, you're awake." Tears poured down her cheeks but she laughed, and he thought he must be going crazy. "Oh, Mitch." She kissed him full on the lips, her mouth warm and sweet, the tears salty. With the one arm he could move he grabbed at her, ran his hand up and down her back to make sure she was real, all the while he drank of her kiss, keeping his eyes open so he could gaze at her wonderful face.

She cupped his cheeks in both hands, pulled back long enough to babble some words he wasn't sure he understood, then began to kiss him all over until his face and neck were wet.

He tried once again to say her name in a voice dry as husks.

"Oh, darling, I'm sorry. Wait, wait just a minute." She pulled away, despite him thinking he had a death grip on her, and was soon back with a dipper of water. She lifted his head and gave him a few sips, holding back when he tried to gulp too quickly.

"I thought you were dead. When I saw you fall I was so frightened. Did you see who shot you?" All this poured out as she fed him the cold, delicious water.

He drank and took in her every expression, the delicate lift of the fine brow, the wrinkle of her exotic nose, the sweep of the long black lashes. When he had enough, he pulled back from the dipper and swept it away with one hand, spilling the last few drops on himself and pulling her close again.

"Don't go. Don't leave. Ever, ever again," he said into her

fragrant neck. Then he was falling, reaching up to hang on. Falling into blackness.

"I didn't leave you, Mitch. You left me," she whispered, but he couldn't hear her.

When he awoke again later in the morning, together they were able to get him into the bed, where he remained the rest of the day.

Ritter came up along about noon and brought her some soup Crane had made from a tough old hen. She asked him in to tell him about Mitch, going into great detail to explain what had happened the night before.

"My God, Miss Charlie. Storm must have covered the sound of the gunshot. Who would have done a thing like that right at our doorstep?"

"Anyone. You know that. But most probably one of Dunkirk's men."

"He's wanted for murder. Could have been anyone who wants the bounty."

She studied him thoughtfully for a moment. "Maybe, but if so why didn't they come on down and claim the body?"

"Probably didn't want to face you," Ritter quipped. "Smart. I'd a shot the bastard, no matter who it was."

"See what I mean?" Ritter said. "How is he, will he be all right?"

She shrugged. "It's clean. Who knows? You know what bullet wounds can be like. Some live, some die, even after you think they're okay. Oh, Ritter, I couldn't bear it if he died."

Ritter stared down at his boots, soaked from the snow he'd waded through. "Well, one thing's for sure, with the snow drifted like it is, it's liable to be a while 'fore anyone shows up for him."

"I won't let anyone take him."

"Even if it's the sheriff?"

She snorted. "Sheriff. That's a joke."

"Still, he is the law." Ritter watched her closely, believing she meant what she said. She was obviously in love with the gunslinger who lay there in her bed. He had watched them together, knew something was up, but hadn't thought it quite this serious. Miss Charlie seemed old enough to know better than to fall for a man like that. But, as he well knew, you didn't get to pick who you fell in love with. It just sort of happened.

Sadly, sometimes there wasn't anything you could do about it, either. "What are you going to do?" he asked.

"As soon as he can travel, I'm getting him out of here. Somewhere where no one will ever find him."

He nodded. Somehow he'd expected that. "What about you?"

"Me?" she asked, gazing at the sleeping man in her bed.

"You can't go on the run with an outlaw."

She gritted her teeth and didn't say anything else.

After a while Ritter excused himself. "I'll bring up some more soup later on, maybe you can get some down him. It'll be good for him."

"Ritter?" she said when he swung open the door. He waited.

"Don't tell anyone he's here."

"Not even Yancey?"

"Not even Yancey. This is between you and me. Promise?"

He fingered his hat a minute, then screwed it down on his head in preparation for going out into the bitterly cold, cloudy day. He twisted to look her in the eye. "I promise, Miss Charlie."

He stepped out onto the porch and pulled the door shut firmly behind him. He'd promise her anything. He'd do anything for her. He couldn't help loving her any more than she could help loving the outlaw. It was just the way things happened sometimes. The godawful way things happened.

Six

It was long after dark when Mitch came awake, strangely alert and rested. Charlie lay curled into his left side, her warm backside tucked against the curve of his hip, her head on his arm. He rubbed his nose in her hair and thought about loving her forever, just like this. Waking up every morning to watch her sleeping next to him. Entering her as she slept, making slow, warm, easy love while daylight broke around them like some kind of bright magic.

He dragged in a harsh breath and held his eyes closed on the vision a moment longer. They would never know each other's bodies in such an intimate way. It was too late. Too late for both of them. He had to get away from her. Far away, before someone came and she was caught up in his guilt. Painted with the same brush that blackened his future.

She murmured and stirred, twisted in the bed so that when she opened her eyes they stared into his.

"Good morning," she said, and kissed him as if it were the most natural thing in the world. As if she were used to finding him in her bed.

He held her, squeezed his eyes shut. "Oh, God, Charlie. God." It was not a curse but a hopeless prayer. He knew better than to expect an answer.

"I love you, Mitchell Fallon," she whispered against his mouth, and ran her warm tongue over his lips.

He moaned and a deep-down ache nearly made him cry out. The agony of losing her might well be his undoing.

"Does it hurt?" She had misunderstood, and he let her.

It hurt all right, but the wound in his shoulder was not the cause of it. He flexed his right arm gently and found he could tolerate the jab of quick, slicing pain.

"It's better," he said, and turned away from her expression of devotion. "Is it still snowing?"

"Ah, so you are back among the living." Her tone rang oddly, as if he had hurt her. Better a little now than a lot later.

When he didn't look back at her, she unfolded herself from the bed and went to put wood in the stove. It was chilly in the cabin, the fire only a cluster of glowing embers.

"You need to nail shutters over the windows for the winter."

"Yes," she said absentmindedly. "I didn't expect it to snow so early." "That's the way with this country. You never know what to expect."

She stood near the fire, hands spread in the welcome warmth as the logs crackled to life. She hated what was going on between the two of them. The sudden coldness, the conversation that meant nothing. He hadn't truly returned to her after all.

"What is it, Mitch? What's wrong?" she finally asked when she could bear it no longer.

He avoided her gaze, stared at the wall beside the bed. "Wrong? What's wrong?

Just about everything, I reckon." His voice was still weak, but harsh nevertheless. "We'll figure something out. I meant between us. You and me."

"There is no us. No you and me. There's only you."

"We were going to get married, and then suddenly you're

gone and the next thing I know you're wanted for murder and I don't even know where you are. If you're dead or alive. I love you, Mitch. You love me, I know you do. You came back. We'll go somewhere where they can't find you."

He snorted, made as if to rise, and groaned. "Dammit, that was a mistake, coming back. I've got to get out of here."

She rushed to the bed. "If you want out of here so bad, why'd you return in the first place?" She glared down at him, wanting to pound on him and to hold him close, all at the same time.

"To make sure you were safe. To see you one more time. Hell, I don't know. I just keep coming back, don't I? If I'd followed my inclinations in the first place I wouldn't be within a thousand miles of here—of *you*. We'd both be better off."

"Then why are you? Why don't you just leave?" She clenched her fists, settled for beating on the mattress where she had lain at his side only a bit earlier. Dreaming of him, of his mouth and his hands and all of him surrounding her, enveloping her, soothing her. "Damn you, why don't you just leave?"

She threw herself at him. He grunted at the agony that lanced through his wounded shoulder, then he had his arm around her, holding her close while she cried.

After a few moments her sobbing quieted and she moved her head to kiss his chest, sliding one hand down past his belly button to rest in the curly hairs below.

He gasped sharply and she nibbled at his throat, at his earlobe. "Charlie, please don't."

"I will, I don't care." Her warm breath sent shivers through him, and then her seeking lips found his, her fingers caught in his hair so that he couldn't have pulled away if he had wanted to.

She shifted without breaking the kiss, and hovered over him, her firm breasts, bare beneath the nightgown, brushed at the hairs on his chest.

He cupped her round buttock with his good hand and urged her to straddle him. The quick, frantic movement pulled their mouths apart, but she bent forward so that one breast touched his cheek. He shifted only slightly and took the taut dark nipple between his lips, flicking his tongue against the tip.

She rocked in ecstasy, locking her knees tight against his waist. She couldn't bear it if he stopped kissing her like that.

Nothing had ever felt quite so wonderful, ever.

Wave after wave of sweet warmth radiated from his mouth deep into the very core of her. Pulsating so that she desired it all, everything he had to give, but couldn't stand the thought of taking her breast from his mouth.

He pulled away and she cried out.

Placing his hand flat across her belly he gently shifted her up and back until he could slip inside her sweetness.

And then she was all hot and cold, wet and smooth, joyous and sublimely content, but with a wildness that possessed her, took her out of herself. The world opened, swallowed her into brilliant sunlight and velvety darkness as she rode a shaft of fiery pain that slipped away into an ecstasy that enthralled her with its beauty and passion.

When she came to her senses, lying facedown on his chest, his hand splayed in her tumbled hair, she thought she must have injured the shoulder wound. He breathed in great jagged gulps that sounded like sobs, and when she was able to rise from his grip she saw tears running from the corners of his closed eyes.

"Oh, Mitch, what's wrong? Is it your shoulder? We shouldn't have... Oh, baby." She played her fingertips gently over his flesh, then wiped the tears where they ran down to his ears.

He opened his eyes, still drenched so they looked like mossy woodland pools, deep and dark and green pools, hiding all manner of secrets.

His silence frightened her and she ran a finger over his full lips. "Please say something, darling. Anything."

He swallowed, licked his lips. "I can't. There aren't any words. We are alive and I love you. Even if I never take another breath. You were right all along. If only this once, we had to love each other just this once." He pulled her down and kissed her so tenderly, so sweetly, that she herself wanted to cry with the beauty of it.

She lay with him until he fell asleep, too exhausted to speak further. Then she rose very carefully, washed in hot water from the kettle on the stove, and put on the dress he had bought her so long ago, when they had been planning their life together.

Wearing it made her feel closer to that time when they had thought happiness awaited just around the corner, closer to a life with him. A life, she saw now, that would never be.

She had no idea what would happen next, but whatever it was, it would happen to the both of them. She would not let him leave her again.

Charlie dropped another stick into the stove, shut the door, and turned in time to see the back door swing inward. Crane stood there staring right at her with wide shocked eyes.

"What do you want?" She ran toward him, tried to shove him back outside before he could spot Mitch asleep in the bed. "What are you doing? Get out of here!"

He might as well have punched her in the stomach when he pulled the pistol and pointed it right at her. "Here, girlie. Stop acting like that." He jerked a quick look around the room, saw the man in her bed. "Just like I thought," he yelled and brought up the gun.

She screamed and swung on his extended arm, ruining his aim so that he shot through the floor. The gunshot boomed in the small room, black powder smoke burnt her eyes and nose.

Startled, Mitch came awake and lunged to a sitting position, grabbed his arm and yelled out in pain.

Nearly deaf from the gunshot, Charlie continued to wrestle with Crane.

He backhanded her, but she came right back at him, swinging an uppercut that caught him on the point of his chin and almost knocked him silly. It did loosen the gun from his grasp so that she was able to wrench it away.

She backed off, holding the pistol out in front of her with both hands. "Now. Now, you. You just don't move. What are you, crazy? What's gone wrong with you? We're kin. How dare you bust in here shooting up the place. No, no, don't you move. You just stay right there where you lay."

"What in the hell is going on?" Mitch yelled, staggering to his feet. Amazingly, he remained upright, though he swayed. All he wore was the bottom half of his union suit.

Feet pounded up the porch steps and someone hammered on the door. Voices outside yelled.

"What's going on in there?"

"Miss Charlie, you okay?"

"Open this consarned door before I kick it in."

She kept her eye on Crane, who showed no signs of rising from his position on all fours. He'd obviously never expected her to fight back so desperately and was now having a hard time getting over being belted in the jaw. She backed toward the front door, yelling out at the same time.

"Quit making so danged much noise. I'm coming, and we're all right. Hold your horses, dammit."

By then she had unlatched the door and in tumbled Yancey, Ritter, and Wolf, the latter making as if to kick the now helpless Crane, the other two panting and cussing under their breath. Snow flew from their boots and pant legs, crusted in the white stuff. A jab of icy air came in with them and continued to come in until Charlie finally convinced them to shut the "damned door."

"What in thunderation is going on in here, anyways?" Yancey boomed. "Crane? Miss Charlie? Fallon? What the hell?"

"I can explain—" she began.

Her cousin interrupted. "I was just trying to pay a visit, and she ups and—" Wolf aimed a kick at the prone man's butt and he howled.

"Shut up, Crane," she ordered and gestured toward him with the gun. "What he was trying," she said to Yancey and Ritter, "was to shoot Mitch, and him already wounded and lying in bed asleep. He's crazy. And if he twitches one more time, I'm going to put a bullet between his ugly eyes, kin or no kin."

"Want me to take him out and throw him off a bluff?" Wolf asked in his low-down, husky voice.

Ritter held out a hand. "Now, take it easy, Wolf, and you, too, Miss Charlie. No call to go shooting anyone or throwing him off no damn bluff."

She whirled toward him. "Don't you go trying to cajole me, I'm not your maiden aunt. I'll shoot the son of a bitch if I'm a mind to."

"She will, too," Yancey said with some admiration.

Wolf made a sound that she supposed was amusement.

"And you just keep quiet, too," she told her ramrod. "Let me think."

Everyone shut up, and all eyes turned toward her. She did, after all, have the gun.

After a moment Mitch groaned and sat down on the side of the bed, hard. Charlie poked the gun toward Yancey. "Here, you watch him," she said and went to Mitch's side.

"I can explain if anyone would just let me," Crane

whimpered, acting brave now that no one was pointing a gun at him and Wolf had quit trying to stomp him to death.

Yancey cast Charlie a dark look. "Looks like to me there's a lot more explainin' than your due around here. But we'll start with you. Speak." He glared at Crane and slammed the S&W on the table.

"I got the stew on the fire, and then I got to thinking it would be nice to—well, to visit with my cousin there. Having not seen her to talk with in a while. She used to enjoy my stories of her father and me as boys. Well, anyway, that's all I was doing.

Being cooped up all the time is no fun.

"How was I to know she had—a man—well, in here in her bed, and would have such a mad fit when I caught them. How'd I know she wasn't a hostage?"

"A hostage? Caught us? You dumb little runt." She dragged her angry gaze away from Crane to check out Mitch, who was pale, but otherwise seemed fine. She said softly, "Why don't you lie back down."

"I'm fine. It's time I got out of here, anyway."

"Oh, you're not going anywhere in the shape you're in." That order issued, she turned her attention back to her visitors. "He didn't catch us doing anything, and even if he had, what business is it of his, or yours either?"

"No one said anything," Ritter muttered. She was wearing a damned dress! And had a man in her bed, and looked all sweet and self-satisfied. It was perfectly obvious what had been going on. And it was painfully obvious that it was none of his business, and she would be the first to tell him so if he brought it up. So he didn't.

"Why are you looking at me like that?" she demanded. He might not have said anything, but from the expression on his face, he was thinking it.

He shrugged and glanced at Yancey. "Like what? I didn't say a word, and I didn't look at you anyway."

A little shame-faced, Crane hauled himself to his feet, but kept one eye on his gun on the table and the other on the silent Wolf. He didn't think Yancey had it in him to shoot him in cold blood and Wolf kept looking at Charlie for a clue, so he inched over to the other chair and sat down opposite the man. "Whew, who'd of expected something like her just grabbing me as I come in the door and socking me like that?"

Yancey grinned broadly. "You socked him?" Wolf issued his amused snort again.

"I did, sir. I most certainly did. And I'm about to sock somebody else, too." She glared at each of them in turn.

Crane eased his hand across the table. "If nobody minds, I'm just going to take my gun and go back to the bunkhouse. This whole thing has upset me, and I don't think I want to stay here any longer. I suppose you'll be firing me from my job now," he said to Charlie as his fingers closed about the gun butt.

She studied him awhile, then thought of all the good stews and bread the man was capable of cooking up. "Oh, I reckon not. That is, if you behave yourself and mind your own business. Don't come sneaking around on me anymore. Come up to the front door proper like, knock, and get invited in or not. Anyway, it wouldn't be right to throw you out in this dreadful weather."

Crane stuck the gun in his waistband and nodded. Next time he would be more careful, and he wouldn't worry if he had to shoot her as well as her outlaw friend. She'd pay for humiliating him in front of everyone. He dredged up the sweetest smile he could manage and went scuffling out the door.

"I'll keep an eye on him," Wolf said, and left, too.

Yancey and Ritter stared at Charlie and Mitch, who sat

side by side on the edge of the bed, then both broke out into laughter. In retrospect the situation was funny, but she realized that sooner or later they would want to know what Mitchell Fallon was doing lying wounded in her bed. For now they could all laugh about it. It would be a long hard winter, with few humorous situations, she would wager. It was best to take them where you could get them.

"I'm going to help him get away," Charlie told her two friends some time later after explanations concerning Fallon's presence were out of the way. "And if you're thinking on stopping me, then just leave. Get off this ranch and don't come back."

Ritter studied his boot toes. Yancey picked at the edges of an old cut on his thumb. Neither would look at Charlie. She had talked Mitch into getting back in bed, but he was wide awake and alert, holding her hand as she sat beside him.

"Think what you're doing," Yancey mumbled.

"I *am* thinking."

"If you take his side you'll lose everything you've worked so hard for, that Matt gave his life for. He's wanted for murder, Charlie. *Murder.*"

"He didn't kill anyone, though," she insisted.

"Yes, I have. Plenty of times in the war," Mitch said, surprising them all. "I reckon that wasn't murder or there's a whole bunch of killers running free. I did go after Neddy and Cross for what they did. They shot you, Yancey. And worse. They've done worse. They killed Zeke and Cal, too. But I called them out fair and square. Both of them at once, and they drew down on me and I shot them. Last I looked, that wasn't considered murder. Maybe in New York City, but not in Montana Territory.

"The colonel wants rid of me, and he's got that so-called sheriff in his pocket. It's simple, but I can't beat it."

He squeezed Charlie's hand. "It's long past time I left this place, anyway. I won't have her in trouble for me. I can get out on my own."

She shook her head angrily. "No, you can't. Look at you. You're helpless as a baby rabbit. You wouldn't get five miles in this weather without help. Yancey, they killed Cal, those awful men. We've got to do something."

"All right," Yancey said, slapped his thighs, and got to his feet. "I'll get him out. How's that? I'll take him into high country, he can hole up in a line shack up there. They won't go looking for him, not in this weather. He can finish mending, then take out when he's recovered, when the weather breaks." Yancey watched Charlie for a reaction.

She held Mitch's hand to her lips for a moment, then looked back at Yancey. "You'd do that for us?"

"I'd do it for you—and for Cal and Zeke," the ramrod corrected. "He don't mean nothing to me, one way or the other."

"No," she said firmly. "Then, no."

"What? Why?"

The men echoed the questions and pinned her with three sets of eyes.

"Because if something happened you'd let him die. Or you'd let someone shoot him if it came to him or you. I wouldn't."

"You mean to tell me you'd go up there with him and protect him with your very own life? You'd die before you'd let someone hurt him?" Yancey practically roared the questions.

"I love him," she said so softly the declaration was almost lost in the aftermath of Yancey's shouted words.

"Love him? You love him? How in the hell did you come to that conclusion?" the ramrod asked. He was fairly jumping with anger. "Lying in the bed with him? That ain't love, Charlie, dammit, that ain't love."

"Get out of here," she said. She leaped to her feet. "Out, out. Both of you. Now, now. Go do whatever it is men like you do when you've got nothing better to do. And leave us alone."

"Miss Charlie, dammit."

"No. Even if you were my father, I wouldn't let you treat me like this. And he wouldn't have. He would've understood about love."

Yancey grew red in the face. "Yes, Matt Houston did know all about love. He loved your mother and he loved you. And you're wrong. He wouldn't put up with your shenanigans with no two-bit outlaw. He had good reason for that, too. He was a good man, was Matt Houston. And you should try to live up to that goodness. Not go wasting your life on a no-account who can do nothing for you but give you misery."

Though he drew breath for more ranting, he didn't get the chance. She went at him with both fists, punching and kicking so that he had to protect himself by grabbing her wrists and holding her out of reach.

She stopped the physical attack, but not the verbal. "You shut up. I'm a grown woman. I have a right to choose my happiness without you throwing my father's love in my face. You don't know what he would have thought, and it's not fair for you to put the words there."

He turned her loose. "He charged me with your well-being. I'm sorry if I hurt you, but it's for your own good I say this. Get him out of here. Let me take him out of here and out of your life before it's too late."

Yancey swung to face Mitch then, appealing to his good sense. "If you love her, then do what's right. Leave before you get her hurt bad. Or *killed,* maybe."

Anger grew so dense within her that her ears pounded with a thunderous heartbeat. She balled her fists once again and shouted, "Stop, you stop this instant. This is my life, not yours. Stop running it. Let him be. Let us both be."

Mitch struggled to his feet and went to her, encircling her shoulders and holding her close. She was so angry it frightened him, and he could feel her trembling even as she allowed him to put his arms around her.

"You'd better get out of here," he said to Yancey. "I'll talk to her. Go on now, leave us be. Come on, Charlie. Come on, darlin'. He's afraid for you. Don't you worry.

Everything will be all right. We all love you, we'll work something out."

She buried her face in his chest, sobbing as if her heart were cracking into bits. She felt as if it were. How could she give up the only true love she'd ever known? It wasn't fair, and she was weary to the bone of being alone.

"I said get out of here," Mitch repeated to Yancey without raising his voice.

The tone may have been soft, but its intensity sent Yancey from the room. He left the door standing open for Ritter to follow, which he did, and pulled it closed so quietly it made no sound above the crackling of wood in the stove and her frantic sobs.

It was a long time after the two men left before she would talk to Mitch, and he gave up soothing her with words that sounded empty and useless in the face of what was about to happen. They would part, they must. And his heart ached as badly as hers at the prospect. He held her, caressed her, kissed her.

It was all he knew to do.

Later he tried to get her to eat a can of her favorite peaches he'd found in the cabinet, but she wasn't interested. So he took his time and made a pot of coffee, heated up the leftover chicken soup and ate as much as he could. He would soon need all the strength he could muster, for he couldn't remain on the ranch much longer.

Another day of sunshine and someone would be beating a path to her door looking for the notorious killer. Him. He had to be gone by then. And the trouble was, he felt as wobbly on his legs as a newborn colt.

Seven

It was a fact that working in the Powder Keg, Radine sometimes heard much more than she wanted. But when that McGrew began bragging and making his plans to go after Mitchell Fallon, snowstorm or no, her ears perked up. He was actually going to do it this time, not just drunkenly talk about it. He was going out the next day to the Double H and he had some men agreeing to go with him. They were in the mood for a lynching, and her friend Charlie was in danger.

Later that night she crept from bed and dressed warmly in several layers of clothes. Wearing an old pair of boots she'd found discarded out back of the mercantile, she sneaked from the room and down the outside back stairs. With luck no one would miss her. They'd just think she had decided to spend the night upstairs with a man.

At the livery she charmed old Clutter into loaning her a horse and saddle and set out for the Double H. The snow covering lit the night so she had no trouble seeing her way.

The horse plodded slowly but steadily through the drifts. Several times Radine drew up to check landmarks. She knew if she headed directly toward the highest of three peaks in the far distance and kept the red bluffs always off to her left, she would come to Porcupine Creek. Charlie's ranch lay just above the creek on the far side. She could ride north for a while, and if she didn't find it, double back, keeping to the creek. With luck she would reach the Double H by daybreak. Without luck, she'd either ride off into infinity and freeze to death or be caught by renegade Indians fleeing the army.

Dunkirk's men could even catch up to her, if they were foolish enough to be out in such weather.

Head down, she rode on into the bitterly cold night, remembering that Charlie Houston was the only woman anywhere she could call friend. The woman had always been nice to her. Once Charlie had brought her a whole box of sweet milk chocolates. Said some young dandy had given them to her. Radine had never had a friend who wasn't a whore, she had to do this for Charlie. Had to warn her that come dawn Duffy McGrew and his vigilantes would leave Miles City with only one thing in mind. Hunt down the man Charlie loved and kill him. The mood McGrew was in, God only knew what they would do to Charlie before they took out in search of the gunslinger they called Yank. McGrew had been in rare temper since his lady wife left him. In fact, he'd turned downright ornery, not at all like the gentleman rancher everyone had taken him for. Course word was his father-in-law was dickering with Colonel Dunkirk to sell him McGrew's ranch, and he held the paper, so he could. Radine didn't blame the man for being upset, but she wished he wouldn't take it out on Mitchell Fallon and Charlie Houston.

Through the pair of thin linen gloves, the cold air stiffened her fingers quickly, but she hung on to the reins. Ice had formed in low spots where the afternoon sunshine had melted the snow and the night's plunging temperatures had refrozen it. But the shaggy little mare was surefooted and every bit as stubborn as its rider. Skirting the highest drifts and doubling back to stay on course, she and her mount reached the Porcupine while it was still full dark. Dawn hovered just beyond the horizon, quieting the wolves in their night song.

After crossing the creek, the horse's hooves cracking through the ice so that she was jostled roughly about in the saddle, Radine paused a moment. To her right, north, if she missed the Double H she would come to Colonel Dunkirk's place. But she had no intention of riding that far.

The insides of her legs were chafed even through the union suit and cotton bloomers she wore, and she remembered once again why she hated to ride horseback. No decent lady would ever subject herself to such misery on purpose. She moaned and the little horse stopped.

"No, honey. I didn't say whoa. Come on, giddup." She nudged the mare's sides with her boots and the valiant little horse moved on. By the time the sky turned an icy silver at the eastern horizon it was obvious that she had chosen the wrong direction. Her fingers had no more feeling and she was cold all the way up her legs. Insides quivering from the cold she reversed direction and headed back. She was beginning to feel frightened. Maybe she wouldn't make it. Maybe they'd find her body frozen into some snowdrift come spring thaw. Until then everyone would wonder what had happened to her. They'd go around supposing this and supposing that. And only old Gutter at the stable would know she had ridden out that night. It would be an almighty mystery and become a story folks would tell for generations.

She giggled at her active imagination and rode on, sagging in the saddle, the warmth emanating off the horse all that kept her from freezing to death. She came upon Charlie Houston's cabin just as the first rays of sunlight burst across the snow-strewn land like a magnificent explosion.

Someone *peck, peck, pecked* at the back door, and the persistent noise finally brought Charlie grumbling from the warm bed. Her eyes were swollen from crying, but she was dry-eyed and quietly furious as she crossed the boards in her stocking feet.

She leaned against the panel. "If that's you, Crane Houston, just take yourself off from here. Go away, whoever it is. I'm not of a mind to deal with any of you."

"Charlie, it's me. Radine. Open up, I'm freezing. Hurry."

"Radine? Where in the world—" She swung open the door, reached out to support the woman who sagged to her knees and reached out almost blindly.

Her breath had frozen in crystals on the muffler wrapped around the lower half of her face, and the skin around her eyes was blue. She could not stand on her own, and Charlie supported her to a chair where she knelt and quickly removed the boots and heavy socks from the woman's tiny feet. They, too, were blue.

"My goodness, what possessed you to come out like this?"

Radine rocked with the pain in her feet and hands, her reply muffled by the frozen cloth around her face. Charlie unwrapped that and fetched the spare quilt that she quickly bundled around the poor woman.

"Let's move you over by the stove and I'll stoke up the fire."

"You've got to listen to me," Radine gasped, while Charlie guided her toward the stove and stuck the chair under her. "They're coming after him. They're coming here to find out if you know where he is, and they'll find out, too."

The noise the two made awakened Mitch, and when he propped himself up to peer in their direction, Radine caught sight of him. "Oh, he is here. Oh, no. They'll kill you both. Oh, you've got to get him out of here. Listen, *listen* to me."

Charlie tossed another stick of wood into the stove and went to put her arms around Radine. "Shh, it's okay. Who's coming? When?"

"Last night. In the saloon. McGrew and a bunch of other men—they talked about—about *him.*" She raised a stiff arm, pointed at Mitchell. "How they're going to kill him 'cause the sheriff is too much a coward to ride out and hunt him down."

"Aw, hell," Mitch said and sat up on the edge of the bed. There he paused, grimaced, then lurched to his feet. "I'm leaving. Now. I won't have you hurt by this."

Charlie paused in her ministrations. "Not without me, you're not."

"Listen, you've got to let him go," Radine babbled. "They'll kill you if you go with him."

"It doesn't matter," Charlie said. She rose and went to Mitch. "I love him, he loves me. Nothing else matters. How can I live without him, Radine?" Her voice rose an octave with the question.

Mitch took her shoulders. "Charlie, don't." "Oh, Charlie. Oh, poor Charlie," Radine said.

"Well, it's true." Charlie put her arms tightly around Mitch's waist. "I love you, and I won't sit here and watch you ride off to be gunned down somewhere, and I won't even know where."

"This is your home, you have to stay here and be safe."

"I don't care about—*this*—anymore. It's not my home, and it's no longer even safe. It belongs to Matt Houston."

"It belongs to you."

"I know and I promised him. It was his dream forever, mine, too. But, Mitch, what I do know is that I don't have anything without you. Empty, I'd just be an empty shell."

Mitch cupped the back of her head with a big palm and pulled her close to his chest. "Oh, Lordy, girl. I know, I know. But I can't let you go with me. I know how that is, and I won't do it. Not again."

"Mitch," she said into his bare chest. "Do you love me?" "Oh, dear God, girl, you know I do."

"Then don't leave without me. Don't leave me here alone. I'll not be alone anymore. I'd rather die with you than stay here alone and always be without you. I swear I would."

"No one is going to die, Charlie. No one. But you've got to let me go." He cleared his throat, gazed down into her dark, tear-misted eyes. "If you go with me they'll catch us. You'll slow me down. I'll be too afraid for you. It'll get us both killed." He swallowed hard, turned away to keep her from reading the truth in his eyes. He expected to be killed and didn't want her to see it.

She sorted her thoughts. If she went to him later, after he was safe, that would work.

"All right, get dressed," she said at last. "Yancey will do what he said in the first place, take you to the line shack in high country. There's food and water there, and wood and a place to sleep. Then he'll come back here, like nothing had ever happened. We'll all say we don't know where you are, haven't seen you. I can make them believe me. Everyone respects me.

"And then when they don't find you, and they won't, I'll come to you. The weather will get worse and they'll give up looking after a while. And when they do, I'll come to you and we'll go away somewhere. Start a new life. It's the best I can do, Mitch. I won't just tell you good-bye and never see you again. And you can't go alone, not in your condition. You wouldn't get there. You'd never make it alone."

He sighed, glanced once at the poor waif wrapped in a blanket by the stove. She gazed back at him with wide moist eyes, shaking her head up and down, up and down. He read her promise there, a promise to see to the woman he loved.

"Yes, all right. But I'd rather Wolf went with me. That's best. He's tough and mean and single-minded. Dammit, Charlie, don't put your life at risk for me. If something happened to you because of it I'd never be able to stand it."

She tilted her face up to look into his eyes, bottomless with anguish, regret, pleading, and saw what she was doing to him. "Oh, my love," she said and touched the scar.

He leaned down and kissed her, transmitting in that kiss all the longing and devotion she'd waited a lifetime for. She felt a tear fall from his cheek to hers and knew she would have to be stronger than she'd ever been. She had to do it for him because she loved him more than herself and because he loved her more than life.

Reluctantly she pulled from his embrace. "Get dressed. Quickly. I'll fetch Wolf.

We'll have you long gone by the time those vigilantes get here. They'll find nothing but me and Yancey and Ritter and our poor old cook, waiting out the winter storm. Now hurry, Mitch. Hurry, please."

In the barn while Ritter saddled the black for Mitch, Charlie rattled instructions to a solemn-faced Wolf, who had agreed eagerly to help.

"After he's safe, you can ride back out the same trail. Drag out your tracks as you come. If you're not back soon and anybody asks, we'll just say you're on a hunting trip. Up in the mountains. For elk or something. I don't know."

"Wolf," Yancey pitched in. "Just tell 'em he went hunting wolves. Everyone knows how them sons a bitches drag down our calves. We sent him wolf hunting, if anybody asks."

She nodded. "And nobody here has seen Mitch, not for weeks and weeks. Not since before we left for Cheyenne." She glared at Ritter who nodded grimly.

"Charlie, honey," Yancey said. "Calm down. Everything will be all right. He'll take care of him. Ain't nothing going to happen." He hesitated a moment, gazed at her with love in his eyes. "I'm so sorry. About yesterday...you were right, I had no call to treat you like a child. It's just, well, I love you."

She touched his arm. "I know. It's all right. And I love you, too." She turned to the silent big man who was busy saddling a large gray for himself. "Please take care of him. Please. He's— he's my life. Do you understand?"

Wolf nodded.

Yancey patted her shoulder awkwardly. "I think I do, too, honey. Matt loved you with all his heart. And he loved your mother even more."

"Never mind that now. This isn't the time. It's Mitch who is important here, not me.

Wolf, I trust you to take good care of him."

All the while they talked, Mitch stood straddle-legged in the wide-open barn door, his back to them while he stared out into the distance. He might as well not have been present, the way they discussed him. Charlie had a habit of taking charge that might rankle some. Mitch found it oddly soothing, for it told him she could handle most any situation without falling apart. He certainly hoped that to be true, for she would need that strength in the upcoming days and weeks when his past was bound to come to light. He wished now they'd had more time together, that he had told her all the things she was bound to hear from others who wouldn't know the whole story.

Wolf yanked at the latigo and tightened down the saddle, dropped the stirrup and climbed aboard.

Mitch turned to see Charlie standing there looking at him with an expression of sadness so intense he wanted to grab her up and take her with him. Kiss away the hurt, love away the pain he'd caused her. He reached out, went to her.

"Mitch," she cried in a small voice and threw herself into his embrace, hugging him so tightly he winced.

She kissed the tip of his chin, his cheeks. "Take care, don't you let anything happen to yourself. I'll come to you as soon as I can."

"Charlie, I don't—"

"Hush," she said and covered his lips with trembling fingertips. "As soon as it's safe, I'll be there. Don't you go riding off anywhere else, you hear? You wait for me."

He nodded.

She stood on tiptoe and kissed him once more quickly, then squeezed her arms fiercely around his neck and buried her face in his warmth for a split second. When she backed off so he could mount she noted that despite his wound, he managed to climb on the stallion without help. It made her feel better about his chances.

Wolf had spurred his horse from the barn and waited outside. Both men carried large bedrolls and double saddlebags loaded with food and water. They would be fine. Charlie just kept telling herself that as she stood in the open doorway of the barn and watched them ride off, headed west toward the Bighorn Mountains. She held her fingers tightly over her mouth to keep from crying out until they disappeared into the thick grove of pine and were gone from sight.

Ritter shuffled a foot on the dirt floor. "I reckon we'd better git Miss Radine hid real good 'fore that bunch gets here. They'll suspect if they find her here. And make sure you clean up all sign of Fallon in the cabin."

She nodded. "Yancey, why don't you ride out behind Wolf and Mitch and obliterate their prints if they leave any. We don't want anyone following them right off this place. What about Crane? Will he talk? He was pretty put out at me yesterday."

"I'll cut his tongue out for him, too," Ritter mumbled. "No, he won't talk. I believe Yancey had a little talk with our friend Crane last night. Made a believer out of him. You ought to get rid of the man, Miss Charlie. There's something about him I just don't cotton to either."

"But he cooks a mighty fine biscuit, Ritter," she said in an attempt at humor. Ritter only nodded, and neither smiled.

"They'll be okay, won't they?" she asked outside the barn.

"Wolf will see to it. And that Fallon. He's one tough fella. He's survived more than this, a lot more. I don't think you need to worry about anything but dealing with that bunch of vigilantes. And I'll be right here with you for that.

"Now, you go fetch Miss Radine and we'll hide her out here in the root celler till they're gone."

They stood there a moment and watched Yancey ride out to do some trail muddying, then Charlie went to get Radine.

As it turned out, the first visitor that day was not the gang of vigilantes that Charlie had expected. Along about ten, Colonel Hulbert Dunkirk showed up accompanied by a new bodyguard even bigger and uglier than Wolf.

She met them in the yard with a loaded Winchester, pointed the thing up at him in his fancy carriage. "Don't bother to light, Dunkirk."

With the wave of a pudgy hand the colonel signaled the ugly man to stay put and addressed her.

"I think you'll welcome what I have to say. I've come to make you a final offer on the ranch. A very generous offer, I must say. Get you out of this hellhole and back to civilization with cash to spare."

"I'm not interested."

"Now, look here, Miss Houston. You and I both know you just barely broke even in Cheyenne. It's liable to be several years before you make enough for a new dress."

"Why, Colonel, I thought you noticed. I'm not much for dresses. Now git. It's cold and I'm tired of standing out here."

At that moment came the thunder of hoof beats, and they all turned to see a handful of mounted men headed for the ranch.

"Looks like the thaw has brought out all kinds of vermin," Dunkirk remarked. He stood and hailed the leader. "You men ride in from Miles City? How's the trail?"

"Dunkirk, what the hell you doin' out here?" Duffy McGrew shouted and vaulted down from his horse.

"I might ask you the same. Shouldn't you be seeing to your own place? Or has Stallings stole it out from under you already? Perhaps he's considering my offer as pretty fair, since he's saddled with a son-in-law like you."

Charlie welcomed the exchange, aware that any delay of the vigilantes meant Yancey, Wolf, and Mitch were that much farther away. Finally she interrupted.

"Gentlemen. Gentlemen, excuse me." They continued to argue and she pulled off a high shot aimed at the distant trees. The resounding blast gained their immediate attention.

"That's better. Now, this is my place, and if you've got a bone to gnaw I'd appreciate you're doing it elsewhere. Could I ask what you want, McGrew? Surely you didn't ride out to argue with Colonel Dunkirk here, seeing as how he's trespassing, too."

"We're on the trail of that outlaw. The sheriff don't see fit to do nothing but prop his feet up on a table in the Powder Keg, and so we figured we'd just do his job for him. There is a bounty on the man's head. Time we cleaned up the territory, we figger."

"And what outlaw might that be?" Charlie asked, her tongue thick and dry. "That Yank fella. Mitchell Fallon, the one marked like a skunk. He's wanted for gunning down Dunkirk's men. Cross and Neddy. Cash bounty on his head."

"Sounded like a fair fight to me," she said. "It's not usually the law's affair when a bunch of gunslingers go at each other. So why the bounty?"

"Because the man is a war criminal." Colonel Dunkirk sputtered. "He's a *what?*"

"Wait a minute, here," she shouted. "First off, I haven't seen hide nor hair of this Fallon since I went to Cheyenne. He lit out over a month ago for Idaho. Second of all, where do you get your information? A war criminal? If that were true the army'd be on his trail, not a bunch of ragged tails like you. So why don't you just ride on about your business."

"I believe we'll just search the place."

She shifted the barrel of the rifle so it was pointed at McGrew's midsection. "You'll not search my place, sir. I don't harbor criminals."

"Yeah, and you don't lay with them either, do you, Miss Charlie?" McGrew said with a sneer.

The men riding with him guffawed loudly, but the noise was cut off when she fired a shot between McGrew's feet. Snow and ice sheared off in all directions and Duffy hopped backward.

In an even, tightly controlled voice, she said, "Not because you say so, but because I want you to be satisfied I'm not harboring any criminals, I invite you to search every building on the place. In my home, you will kindly wipe the mud off your boots and keep your filthy hands out of my things. It's one room, you can see real quick that no one's there. Now, git busy so you can git off my place."

She trailed along with smug satisfaction while the men went from barn to bunkhouse to cookhouse and finally to her cabin. Idly she wondered where Crane had gotten to. There was no sign of him anywhere.

After McGrew and his men left, she faced the colonel. "I don't know exactly what you're hanging around here for. You might as well ride on your way. I've told you, my place isn't for sale. And even if it were, I wouldn't sell it to you if I were starving. I'd give it back to the Indians first. So you and your hired killer get off my land and don't come back. Next time I see you on my property I'll put a bullet in that fat gut of yours just to see if you bleed red blood."

Dunkirk's mouth dropped open with astonishment. He nodded curtly to his driver/bodyguard and they were off in a flurry of ice and snow and mud.

When she turned to go back toward the cabin she saw Crane lurking in the doorway of the cookhouse. Where had he gotten to earlier?

She dismissed all thought of her cousin when Ritter brought Radine back to the house in a few minutes, straw clinging to her hair and clothes.

"They never even found the trapdoor to the root cellar. Good idea to put her down there," he told Charlie proudly.

"Thank you very much, Ritter," Radine said sweetly and patted the young man's cheek. He blushed furiously and stammered his way from the cabin.

"I believe that fella needs a woman to teach him a few things," Radine said as she settled once again close to the stove.

"He is a shy one, but I don't know what I would have done without him. He understands things the other men don't."

"And he loves you," Radine added. "No."

"Yes, indeed. But you don't need to worry. He's so in awe he won't ever try to do anything about it. He'll just worship from afar."

"That's so sad," Charlie said softly. "To love someone and not be able to—able to do anything about it."

"It happens to a lot of us," Radine said.

Charlie swallowed over a lump in her throat. Somewhere out there in the drifts of snow and bitter cold rode the man she would always love, going farther and farther away from her with every passing hour. Would she ever see him again? How would she live without him? Yet another cold and lonely winter awaited, with little hope for happiness. This was such a vast country. Its wide-open spaces, the infinite miles of land and mountains and sky lent to the feeling of her own tenuous existence.

And yet she knew that she and Mitch, Radine, Yancey, Ritter—*everyone*—were important bits and pieces of the whole, threads in a fabric that held this immense country together, for better or worse.

She sighed and went to sit beside Radine. Sometimes she just got much too sentimental for her own good.

"Can you cook?" she asked Radine.

"Some. I'm not fancy, but I can stir up meat and potatoes, beans and coffee, corn pone and biscuits."

"Well, then. Would you teach me? It seems we have some time on our hands."

"I would be delighted," Radine said. "But I really ought to go back to Miles City.

Lance will be wondering what happened to me."

"You won't get fired if you stay awhile, will you?"

Radine threw back her head and laughed. "I never was hired, far as I know. We have a—well, let's call it a working arrangement. He don't pay me, I don't pay him. It's a bargain that fits both of us."

"Well, then. Stay awhile. Teach me to cook and I'll see you have room and board with me. How would that be? Oh, please do. I'd love having you. It's so lonely out here, and the men have their own things to do." Charlie pondered what she'd said for a moment or two. "Funny, there was a time I'd a been down there in the bunkhouse playing cards and matching the men tale for tale while we sat around the stove. I don't have much of a hankering for that anymore."

Radine smiled "Maybe you're turning into a proper lady. That's what love does to you. Makes you think of birthing babies and cleaning house and… and cooking." She eyed Charlie from under half-closed lids. "And of course, the very best part. The loving part."

Charlie felt a flush, but joined her in easy laughter. How good it was to relax and enjoy company, even if just for a short while.

Eight

Someone knocked loudly on the door and Charlie picked up the rifle from its niche before opening it. She'd heard no one ride up. Slipping the latch she poked the barrel through the crack and peered at Crane Houston.

"What do you want?"

He smiled. "To visit, that's all." "What about?"

"Wasn't that long ago you enjoyed my telling you stories about your dad when we was kids." He waited.

"That what you want to visit about. My dad?"

"Well, that and something else. It's real important. It's about your mother and something you might want to know. We all want to know about family. I figger...no, I know you're no different."

"You knew my mother, too?"

He shrugged. "In a manner of speaking."

She let the door swing wider. Even Matt hadn't been too forthcoming about her mother. Besides, Crane wasn't armed and she was.

After she let him in she propped the rifle in the corner nearby. Handy just in case. Then she seated him at the table and took the other chair for herself, without offering coffee. The house smelled of good cooking, and she was proud of the bread and spice cake Radine had helped her create the day before. She didn't offer any to Crane. She was still pretty mad at him.

He picked nervously at the tip of a callused thumb, finding it hard to get started with whatever he'd come to say.

"Well?" she finally asked, a bit curtly.

"Well? Well. Your ma was a pretty woman, young. Sixteen, I believe when you were born."

She nodded. That she knew. Where was this going?

He turned his head and slanted his eyes at her slyly. "He ever tell you how they met?"

She searched her memory, Matt's flowing descriptions of the Florez hacienda, her own recollections that were merely tiny flashes that she couldn't ever put together, she'd been so young when he came to take her away from her grandparents. Then she shook her head.

"That dirty little shack in El Grande, and her huddled back in the corner, dirty and near naked?"

She blinked and stared at the man. "What are you talking about? My mother was a lady from a fine, rich family. Dolores Maria Ramona Florez. Do you think I'm stupid? What is this?"

On her feet, she prepared to do battle.

He held up a hand. "Hold it, don't go getting snippety on me. It was your mother all right, and she'd been raped until she was of no more use to the banditos who left her there. Your daddy always was a bighearted son of a bitch. He felt sorry for the poor dirty little waif.

"Imagine his surprise when he gets her cleaned up and finds out who she is.

Where did you think he got his bankroll to leave King and go out on his own?"

She nearly spat at Crane. "That's a filthy lie. You get out of here and off this ranch.

Now." The order would barely pass over her dry tongue. This man was infuriating.

He rose to face her, barely tall enough to look her in the eye. "You were the baby she carried in her belly. Sired by some no-account white border bandit who never looked back. Not a child of the almighty Matt Houston at all."

Burning tears filled her eyes, and her heart thumped so hard she couldn't breathe properly. "You lying devil, you evil ugly little man. How can you spout such filth?"

His close-set eyes sparked and he grabbed her arm viciously, swung her around, and popped her soundly on the jaw with his fist. It knocked her to the floor, where she crouched on her hands and knees, shaking her head to clear the flashing lights and a falling curtain of darkness. She gazed at the rifle, just out of reach.

The sound of his oily voice fell all around her. "We're going to talk some more about just what your rights are here on your daddy's ranch. I think we can come to some sort of agreement. What do you suppose people would think? Even if that outlaw Fallon didn't care, which he just might, there's all the other ranchers. Bastards don't have any rights to inheritance, and especially not if they're women. The law won't look kindly on this."

Jaw aching she swung her head, glared up at him. "I don't give a damn what people think. Who's going to listen to your lies, anyway? You get out of here. Mitch will kill you when he finds out. You poor little fool."

"It's you who's the fool, cousin. The next time I'll aim better and your gunslinger will be dead."

"You shot Mitch?"

He nodded, a sardonic grin revealing yellowed teeth. "Who'd you think? That fat toad Dunkirk? He has to hire everything done, but I'm tired of waiting to be paid. We're going to do it the easy way, and the colonel can eat worms."

She struggled to get to her feet, but he shoved her with the toe of his boot so that she tumbled to her butt up against the wall.

"I think we need to discuss a few things here."

"I'm not discussing anything with a liar."

"We'll see who's lying. Where were you living when your... when Uncle Matt came to fetch you?"

"With my grandparents, my mother's parents." She let out the reply before realizing that she didn't want to discuss this.

"And how old were you?" "Five, no four. I'm not sure."

He held his tongue between his teeth a moment. "What happened to your mother?"

The question didn't deserve an answer and she didn't give it one. "She killed herself, didn't she?"

With a quick flick of her eyes, she measured the distance to the rifle standing in the corner near the bed, then glared at him. He mustn't guess her intent.

"I don't suppose you remember her at all, but then you really should. I do and I'm only a couple years older than you."

What was he getting at? She tenderly massaged her throbbing jaw.

"Oh, your 'daddy' married her all right, but only for the money. They paid that no-account Matt Houston to marry their precious daughter and claim her bastard. You. And then there you were, and for a while Uncle Matt, well he just took off. Oh, he come back all right, after she was dead. It was big talk in the family. My dad ranted and raved about his only brother taking that Mexican bastard on just so's he could get the money he needed to start out on his own. Uncle Matt had learned all he could from Richard King, but he never saved enough money for a spread of his own. He had too much liking for high-stakes living at the poker tables in San Antone."

Nearly blind with fury, she used the energy of the adrenaline surging through her veins to catapult from the floor and leap for the rifle. The tips of her fingers skinned across the polished stock just before he grabbed her and tossed her aside.

Standing over her, he shook his head. "Naughty, naughty. Why do you think you never went back to visit your grandparents, or they never came to see you in Texas? Because they wanted nothing to do with their daughter's shame, that's why. She killed herself, your mother did. Out of humiliation for what she had done. Leaving them you to look at day after day. A terrible reminder."

"She did nothing, nothing," Charlie screamed. "Even if it was true, she wasn't to blame."

"Ah, but it is true, and you're beginning to believe me, aren't you? It all fits together, doesn't it? Daddy suddenly buying that big spread, the cattle and horses and fancy house and servants. Did you really think he earned that kind of money working as a lackey for Richard King?" Crane shook his head pityingly. Then he leaned forward and took her chin in an iron-hard grip.

"Pretty little Mexican bastard. A Texas bandit for a father and a whimpering little Mex for a momma. You're not a Houston. Look at you. Just look and tell me you see anything of Matt Houston there. Hell, all the white blood in the world won't make you anything but a no-account greaser."

She gritted her teeth against his painful grip on her jaw. Though she wanted to spit in his eye, all she could do was stare at him through a misty haze of hatred. He was lying, he had to be. She couldn't *think.*

Everything was blurred, his hateful face, the bed, the stove, the table and chairs, the Winchester out of reach in the corner. What was going on here, what did this man want? All she knew for sure was that if he ever took his eye off her for a second she would grab up the Winchester and blow him to kingdom come. She might even laugh as she did it.

But Crane wasn't about to give his cousin that chance. "Where are the papers on the place?"

She shook her head, then wished she hadn't, for everything went fuzzy again. "What? What papers?"

"The deed on this place. The Double H. By rights it belongs to me, the only heir of Matt Houston. You're gonna sign it over to me."

"No, I won't You mangy, no-good liar. I'll never do that. You'll have to kill me." "Oh, no. If I could get it by killing you you'd be dead already. But Dunkirk would have it then, faster than I could say brown mule, and I wouldn't see a dime. I want it all legal and proper."

"Legal and proper? You call this legal and proper, forcing me? Coming in my home and knocking me around like the low-life coward you are? You're crazy, that's what you are."

He shrugged. "I guess I could beat you till you did what I wanted, but that might look suspicious if you went to the law. So I reckon I'll just have to play my ace in the hole, my draw card, the one I've kept up my sleeve. Uncle Matt would appreciate this, he truly would."

He pulled back the tail of his coat to dig in the inside pocket. He was distracted just enough for her to scramble away from him. Grunting she clawed her way to the rifle.

She whirled, both hands wrapped firmly around the breech. Crane shouted and pounced. But she had moved just out of his reach, and this time she had a better grip. The barrel punched him right in the belly. He grabbed it, wrapped his hands around hers, and as they struggled, fingers clawing around the trigger guard, the gun went off.

The explosion kicked her backward into the wall, its blast

slamming into her eardrums. Thick acrid black powder smoke choked off her breath, tears poured from her burning eyes. For a moment she stared with disbelief, the blast echoing around the tiny room.

He didn't let go of the rifle barrel, just stood there hugging it while he let out a low bawling sound like a downed steer. He tottered there for what seemed an eternity, then crumpled to the floor where he lay motionless, a look of stark amazement frozen on his features.

She'd killed him!

She did nothing for the longest time but stand over him and gape. Her eyes blinked, adrenaline pumped through her system like boiling acid—her mouth dried to paper around the remaining taste of black powder. Her heart boomed like echoes of the gunshot. Still she couldn't move from the spot.

Blood spread in a thick pool around the body before she finally came to her senses.

She tugged at the stock of the Winchester until his death grip gave up the barrel.

With frantic choppy moves she went to her knees beside the bed, dragged out her father's metal box of important papers. In it was the deed to the Double H Ranch. Her fingers bumped up against the music box and she pulled it out, too, making a double bundle out of the two with a blanket from the bed. She had to run, get away, go to Mitch. Quickly she put together a bedroll of her heaviest clothes, filled a cloth sack with food from the larder, and picking up the Winchester headed for the barn. She spared not even a glance at her dead cousin.

Just like Mitch, she would be judged a killer and an outlaw. She would find Mitch and they would go away together. Far away where no one would ever find them. What else could be expected from the bastard child of a bandit?

Snow began to fall late in the afternoon, spitting at first, but then saturating the air in a thick impenetrable blanket of fat flakes, some as large as wild plum blossoms.

Charlie hunched deeper into her woolen coat, stopping once long enough to shake out the canvas poncho and wrap up in it. Surely this early blizzard wouldn't continue through the night. That reasoning soon proved to be a fallacy, for the farther she rode, the sorrel picking its careful way as they climbed into high country, the harder the snow fell.

It most certainly could snow all night. Could she find the line shack if it kept up? She had always been proud of her unerring sense of direction. As afternoon darkened into evening she began to look for a place to make camp for the night. Not even the best Indian trackers would ride on in a blizzard after dark.

Yet nothing mattered but that she catch up with Mitch. Not the horror of what had happened in the cabin, nor the terrible stories Crane had spouted about her father.

The first night she camped under an overhang that extended almost deep enough to be a cave. She was safe from the worst of the raging wind, but not warm enough to be comfortable. The shelter was big and would shelter both her and the sorrel. Once she had a fire going and the blanket, coat, and poncho wrapped around her, she felt safe from freezing during the night.

What would Ritter do when he returned to the ranch to find her gone and Crane gut shot? Suppose Yancey returned as well. Was Mitch already safe in the line shack?

Before she found answers a weary sleep pounced on her like a hidden beast. She dreamed then of Mitch, his lips nibbling her fevered flesh, passion smoking his green eyes, and of Matt Houston, the fair skin and aquiline features, sandy hair and brittle cobalt eyes. She thought he pointed at her, but saw that instead he shook his finger at a hazy, dark-skinned man whose teeth were bared in laughter. When she whirled to get a better look the man became her. Her face, her naked body, sprawled on a dirt floor, mouth opened in a soundless scream.

She cried out and awoke herself, startled the sleeping horse so that he snorted and pawed.

The snow had stopped and the sky glowed like polished gunmetal. False dawn. She could sleep no longer and rose, rubbing her tingling muscles and stomping the ground to bring feeling into her legs and feet. She filled a tin cup with snow and pushed it into the glowing coals, stacking more dry wood on the fire at the same time. When the water was hot, she sprinkled its surface with dried sassafras bark and let it steep.

She would need energy, and so added a healthy dose of dark sugar for good measure.

Standing hunched over the dying fire she washed down a slab of spice cake with the tea. After doling out a ration of feed to the horse, she packed up and moved on. A need to reach Mitch drove her so that she ignored the cold wind that cut eerie shapes in the new snow and brought tears to her eyes, exposed above the muffler she'd wrapped around her mouth and nose. Beyond the scudding clouds the sun broke through and glared off the white drenched land in shards of painful light that almost blinded her.

She squinted, spotted the familiar gap ahead that would lead her into the hills and ultimately to the line shack. Beyond the rising land the indigo and purple mountains stood like giant guardians. She halted the horse a moment, twisted in the saddle, and glanced back the way they had come. Her past chased her, reached out and grabbed at her, urging her to return to where she belonged. She gasped for air and pulled the muffler away from her face. Great clouds billowed from her mouth, were caught by the wind and dissipated. She could die out here, frozen to death, and maybe never be found.

She considered that for only an instant, then turned back toward the rugged hills thick with towering ponderosa and lodge pole pine and blue-green spruce.

To break the uncanny silence, she spoke aloud. "Oh, God, Mitch, I love you." The words bounced around in the cold air, darted back at her in echoes that faded away to nothing. High above her a hawk screed in reply, and she shaded her eyes to search the pale blue sky.

McGrew had called Mitch a killer, but it wasn't true, it couldn't be. What Mitch had done, he had done for good reason, and she would never believe him to be a cold-blooded killer. Not any more than she could think of herself that way because of what had happened to Crane. But folks would all say it was so. How easily a thing like that could happen. How quickly life could explode around you, so that nothing tangible and dear remained. Nothing but the man in the line shack up there somewhere, a man who was all she had left in this world to cling to.

The weary gelding cut the trail to the line shack by late afternoon, but they would not make their destination before dark. That meant another night spent out in the open. The heavy snow had slowed their passage, they had waded drifts so deep that at times she had dismounted and led the valiant horse. With relief she saw that the trail was blown clear in most places. It snaked around the outer perimeter of the ridge with a sheer drop off to the left, and was still treacherous, with icy patches and loose shale. It was there, as the animal picked carefully through the clattering rock, that he lost his footing and fell. Hooves rattling for purchase in the slick gravel, he screamed and lunged, trying to keep all four legs under him. But his hindquarters went down. She kicked loose of the stirrups and bailed off just as he plunged over the edge.

Frantically she crawled to the rim and peered down, heart hammering thickly in her throat. The horse lay several hundred yards below on a wide shelf. He kicked once, nickered, and then didn't move again.

She had to get down there. Without her bedroll she would never make it through the frigid night. She would freeze to death. Before she could lose her nerve, she twisted around on her stomach, let her legs dangle over the precipice, and poked around with her booted toes until she found a solid foothold. With gloved hands she latched on to a sapling pine and lowered herself another few feet. Slowly, agonizingly, inch by inch, she worked her way down to where the sorrel lay. Once or twice she slipped in the snowy terrain, but always dug in and held on.

It was dark by the time she touched both feet to the wide ledge where the horse lay unmoving. Panting and exhausted she gazed at the gelding through tears she told herself were from the cold. But down deep inside she knew they were for Mitch and herself, for the poor animal, and for the loss of her father and Cal. So much death, such sadness. She slipped off one glove and touched the cooling flesh of the horse. Dead.

She'd known that already. Anger and a stubborn will to survive brushed away her tears. No time now, dammit, no time for weakness. It could get her killed.

The blanket in which she had tied up the strongbox and the music box weren't on the horse, they must have come off in the fall. The rifle, too, was missing. She would search in the morning. The bedroll she unfastened and tossed up against the cliff face. One of the saddlebags was caught partway under the heavy body and she strained and heaved, muscles bulging, before she finally yanked it free of the animal's dead weight. Sweat had soaked through her clothes by the time she set up a makeshift camp against the cliff behind the body of the gelding.

She made a small fire of pine branches scrounged from the bluffs face and snuggled down in her wrappings, chewing on a piece of mangled spice cake from the saddlebag.

The next morning she crawled stiffly to where she could stand and tilted her head to gaze up the sheer precipice toward the trail. Hard to believe she had come down that, and now all she had to do was climb back up.

When he returned from taking Radine to Miles City Ritter drove the team straight into the barn and unhitched them. The house appeared deserted and still, and he decided to check on Charlie. The door to the cabin fell open under his fist and his heart thudded heavily. The overpowering stench of gunpowder and a pitiful groan greeted him.

He found Crane sprawled in a pool of thickening blood and hurriedly knelt beside him. "What happened? Where's Miss Charlie?"

"Shot—me. Shot—gone."

The rattle of hooves outside heralded another arrival, and Ritter postponed the questions to hurry to the door and greet Yancey. Disregarding the cook's obvious pain, the two hailed each other.

Yancey stomped inside and glanced around. "What in thunderation's goin' on in here? Where's Charlie?"

"If I know'd I'd tell you," Ritter said. "This son of a bitch, he knows. Now help me beat it out of him."

Yancey slammed the door and knelt down opposite Ritter. "Who shot him?"

"He says Miss Charlie."

Crane nodded, then groaned some more.

"If she did, well then I reckon she had good reason," Ritter said. "Blamed well told she did," Yancey said.

"Aw, he ain't hurt bad. Dang bullet just barely cut through the flesh. Too bad it wasn't a tad to the left, we'd a not had to worry none about this one. I reckon this here blizzard helped you wipe out them tracks just fine. Where you been?"

Yancey shrugged, stared out the window for a while. "Had to hole up till the worst blew over. I come the long way around so I wouldn't run across any of them yahoos. It was snowing my tracks full most of the way. Don't figure there's any danger anyone can follow them to the line shack at Redrock—it's rough country."

Before Ritter could chastise Yancey for saying anything in front of Crane, the thunder of approaching horses sounded.

"Well, dang," Ritter muttered, and went to peer out the window. "It's that Duffy McGrew and his crew of vigilantes, and he's got some of the colonel's men with him, and, aw hell, there's the sheriff, too."

"Fine pairing," Yancey said. "You reckon they're looking for Fallon?"

"I expect they are. They rode off after all of you yesterday not long after you left."

Yancey grunted. "Didn't get too far, did they? And where was you when this happened?" He gestured toward the man on the floor.

"I took Miss Radine back to town and the storm come and so I stayed till today. Hell, I couldn't have got back. Who would have thought her own cousin couldn't be trusted to look out after her?"

"Well, you shouldn't have left her alone with him. I figgered that Wolf would be coming back in by now, but he must have laid out the storm, too."

Ritter scowled. "Can't tell about him. Want me to go see what them yahoos want?"

"I expect you'd better, but watch what you say."

Ritter bit back a reply. Yancey ought to know he had better sense than to misspeak in front of that bunch of mavericks.

As it turned out, though, Crane Houston spilled the beans, with Ritter and Yancey trying hard to stop him, while the sheriff and Duffy McGrew stood there taking it all in.

"Well, I expect we need to go after them, then. Fallon and the girl both. These sissies have wasted enough time holed up in town for the storm to blow over," the colonel said after Crane finished his blabbering about Red Rock Canyon and the line shack.

"Figgered we'd find the two of them nice and cozy right here. This storm and all. I reckon it's too late to start today," the sheriff said. "It'll be dark in an hour. We'll leave out first thing in the morning. Everybody pack plenty of food and clothes and ride your best horse."

"Old fool," McGrew muttered where Ritter could hear him. "Think he was the only one who knew this country. He'll probably fall off his horse drunk 'fore we even get out of sight of Miles City."

"You two men can go with us," the colonel said to Ritter and Yancey.

"Not me," Ritter said. "I ain't tracking down Miss Charlie."

Yancey punched him in the shoulder, shook his head. "Course we're going.

Wouldn't miss watching you durn fools chasin' your tails all over them mountains for a few days. It oughta be good fun. Now, who's gonna take this fool back to town to the doc's? Won't be me, I'd as soon he died as not."

❀

With one leather-gloved hand Charlie clung to the exposed
root, her cheek pressed tight against the bluff. The pungent
odor of wet earth and sap invaded her nostrils. She wished she
could look up, but didn't dare for fear of falling. Instead she
peeked down and tried to gauge how much farther she had to
climb. Maybe she'd come halfway. It was hard to tell.

Feeling above her head with her other hand, she grabbed
on to another slippery root, tugged hard to test its strength,
and then patiently knocked new toeholds with first one foot,
then the other.

Only a few more feet and she would be able to see over
the rim. She rested a moment, then began the process once
again. It was rough going, especially with the bedroll strapped
to her back. She hadn't found the rifle, nor the bundle holding
the music box and Matt's strongbox. The saddlebags she'd had
to leave behind. No way to carry them. But she figured if she
could climb to the trail by noon, she could walk to the line
shack before dark.

As she struggled for yet another handhold, she imagined the
expression on Mitch's face when she burst through the door and
threw her arms around him. His presence and the warmth that
would pour from the mud fireplace in the tiny shack became so
real as she climbed that heat played on her face, his taste touched
her lips, and her flesh trembled with his imagined caress.

She shivered and inched painfully upward, grunting and
clutching at anything she could find to hang on to. Kicking at a
loose spot to make yet another toehold, she raised upward and
one hand felt something different. A flat spot, smooth rocks.

Was she there?

She patted around a bit and must have moved too quickly,
for one foot slipped free and dangled out in space. She skidded
down, scrabbled and grabbed at something, anything, cried

out as she slid, envisioned plunging back down beside the dead gelding, or worse falling all the way to the bottom of the canyon.

In her crazy descent, a root she grabbed held, and she hung there by one hand taking shallow breaths that burned down into her lungs.

With one foot she carefully felt around for a toehold, found it, and stood upright so that her shoulders were above the trail. The bundled blanket lay right in front of her, still tied around the music box and strongbox. It must have fallen off before the sorrel pitched over the edge.

Nearly sobbing with relief she bent forward and squirmed onto her belly on the trail, legs still dangling over the rim. The chant became a silent prayer of thanks.

She had made it.

Nine

The sun dropped below the jagged cut of mountains off to her left. Breath coming heavy, she rounded an outcropping of sienna boulders and spotted the line shack, nestled back in a grove of pines. It overlooked a vast meadow that stretched out before her, a lake nestled in its midst like a tiny jewel, shoreline iced and sparkly.

Smoke trailed from the chimney of the shack in a thin spiral that flitted among the green-needled tree branches.

Relief swelled through her. She panted out Mitch's name with every step she took.

The expression on his face when she burst inside told her all she needed to know.

With a whoop he kicked away from the chair and wrapped her in his arms before she could even close the door at her back. He smelled of wood smoke and strong coffee. His hand on the back of her head felt strong, gentle, caring.

"Oh, how I missed you," she breathed into his chest.

He hugged her so tightly she gasped, his mouth at her ear, then searching across her cold, cold face to find her lips.

She tasted him, touched him all over, fingers in his hair, along his shoulders, over his back. At last their mouths locked as if starved for the nourishment each could give the other.

"Ah, dear God, you're so cold," he said, and began to undress her.

The hat and bedroll first, then the gloves, poncho, and coat. Rubbing at her arms, pulling her closer to the fire, all the while planting hot quick kisses wherever his lips could reach.

Exhaustion and cold faded and she closed her eyes, gave herself up to his care. Only then did he notice the door ajar, the bitterly cold air invading the small space.

"Wait, don't move. Stay right there." He held out both hands toward her, as if he could fix her in place with some kind of invisible lines. He never took his eyes off her, backing up against the door and shoving it closed.

She saw at last the clarity of his features. The drawn, haggard look of him, as if he had undergone some terrible and tragic experience. Holding out a hand she beckoned him to her side where she sat coiled beside the fire. And he came down to her, gathering her close.

"I thought I'd never see you again. You're here, really here." He touched her face with the tips of his fingers, quick little fluttering touches, then with a shudder he hugged her up close again.

After a while he said, "All this time I hoped you wouldn't come, but prayed for you to with every breath. Why did you? How…?"

"Don't ask, not yet," she begged and turned her face up to study him. "You look so tired. How's your shoulder? Are you eating, looking out for yourself?"

"Yes. No. I don't know. It's all right. It was bad when I first got here, but I slept… I must have slept a long time. I don't know what day it is. I haven't been awake too long, I don't think."

"And Wolf. When did he leave?"

"Lit out right away, tried to beat the storm. I couldn't get him to stay. Odd fellow, fits his name to a tee. Let's not talk about all this." He dropped his head to her shoulder, sighed, and together they lay down in front of the fire. "I just want to hold you. Hold you forever."

"Yes," she said into his neck. "Yes."

She awoke wrapped in his arms, his breath soft and sweet in her hair. "Oh, Mitch," she whispered. "What are we going to do? I love you so much. Oh, Mitch."

He slept on without a reply.

Again she dozed off, and the next time she awoke he was lying just as they had been when she fell asleep, but watching her with moss-green eyes that spoke volumes.

The fire had burned low, and he rose to put a few chunks of pine on the flames.

They sparked and cracked and lit the room with dancing golden light

When he lay back down beside her and took her in his arms, their lips touched, lingered, broke away, and came together once again. They uttered little sounds of pleasure that rippled through the silence like pebbles dropped in a still pond.

Hands found bulky clothing, buttons popped, shirts came away, jeans loosened and peeled down, leaving them both in their under drawers.

He stopped for a moment, studied her lithe frame, brushed the back of his knuckles over her breasts. The nipples puckered beneath the woolen material. Keeping his eyes on her face he began to slowly unbutton the top, stopping after each button to kiss her, first through the rough fabric, taking little nibbles at her breasts, then on the bare skin when the cloth came open down the front. His moist breath heated her skin and she pushed into the love bites, moaning with pleasure.

On his knees, hands at her waist, he buried his face in the

taut mound of her belly. "I only knew how much I loved you when I had to leave you. It hurts so much to be without you. All I want to do is hold you forever."

She took his face between her palms and tilted it so that he was looking at her. "It's all right, we won't have to be apart again. We've got plenty of time. All the time in the world. I've so much to tell you."

He shushed her lips with the tips of his fingers. "Not now. Not this minute. I want you first, I want every inch of you, I want to be in you and around you and with you. All of you. Now, this very moment. Please. Later we'll talk, later." He groaned and ran his hands over her, at the same time nibbling on every inch of exposed skin he could find.

Despite her weariness and despair, her body knew what it wanted. This man, his touch, his kiss, his lovemaking, was all her frenzied flesh desired. Everything else could come later. Much later. His desire, his passion, had chased away everything but their mutual needs. He was alive and so was she, and it would be enough for now.

They should celebrate.

With frenzied desire he peeled off her union suit, she removed his, and soon they were lying naked on the floor in the eerie golden glow from the fire. He raised to one elbow, gazed at her with the firelight sparking in his green eyes, and she touched the scar along his brow line. His dark hair tumbled over her hand. He closed his eyes a moment, as if to shut out unwanted memories. Then he pulled her hand from the scar, kissed the open palm, and gently placed it low on his belly. She caressed the heat and rising manhood, and he lowered his mouth to trail his tongue over her lips, darting its tip in and out in a matching rhythm to her touch.

The warm kisses moved from her mouth down across each

breast beyond the gentle mound of her stomach, heated her longing so she lifted her hips to welcome the sweet deep search.

In her eyes the fire leaped higher and higher, consuming their slick, naked bodies, carrying their ashes into the darkness of night and beyond, shooting their souls into the frigid black sky beyond the stars.

He gathered her into his lap facing him, and entered her with a smooth and tender grace, nudging the core that exploded as they rocked together, crying and laughing and sobbing in ecstasy. He shuddered and stopped moving, holding her close and breathing great gasps against her throat, unmoving except for the rhythm deep inside. Then he let out a gentle "aah" and they lay side by side on the floor once again.

She wasn't sure how they had gotten there, spooned as she was, butt tucked up against the curve of his stomach and thighs. Perhaps she had passed out for a moment or at least lost all conscious thought.

Around and within her rested a serenity as if she had been soothed by an angel, and she tucked his hand close to her heart and slept.

Mitch awoke with a shooting pain through his injured shoulder, and seeing that he and Charlie were sleeping on the hard floor, didn't wonder.

He'd thought it all a dream, the lovemaking and ecstasy of having her, but waking with her hair tousled beneath his chin filled him with an extreme joyousness. It had, after all, been real. No dream could have given that much pleasure. He grinned and shifted, trying to get rid of the ache in his shoulder muscles. Foolish of him to act in such a crazy fashion. Foolish but oh, so wonderful.

He eased his arm from around her and stretched out the worst of the kinks, but couldn't help groaning.

She came awake instantly and sat up, her bare breasts tilted toward him, her eyes wide and frightened. That went away almost immediately when she took in their joint naked condition.

"I thought I was dreaming," she said, and smiled so sweetly he sensed a gentle cracking around his heart. That old, tough and non-caring man gave way to someone else. A man who trusted again, loved again.

"I love you, Charlie Houston, with everything I have to give. And I always will." "Oh, Mitch, I—" Her eyes filled.

"But if I don't get up off this floor I'll be crippled for life. And another thing—" He struggled to his feet, using the back of a chair for help "—what the *hell* are you doing up here, anyway?"

Sitting there on the floor, looking up at his totally naked, beautiful body, his face attempting to scowl away the satisfaction from the night before, she couldn't help but laugh.

"It's not funny, Charlie. You came up here alone and you could have been killed. My God, what were you thinking?"

Everything that precipitated her flight came back in a rush that sobered her quickly. "I have to have clothes on for this," she said. "No more questions till we're dressed, please."

He nodded in agreement, and they both dressed, strangely shy in the small room with no privacy for either. He finished first and stepped outside to gather some wood for the fire. It was snowing again, great fat flakes that had already filled her tracks to the door.

He fanned the coals to life and added a few sticks of kindling. "I'll put on some coffee." Suddenly he wasn't so anxious to have this talk with her. What could have happened to upset her so ?

With his back to her, shoving the pot of water and grounds into the fire, he didn't get a good look at her face when she blurted out her news.

"I killed Crane Houston, Mitch. He's dead and I killed him."

The announcement left him speechless. He turned to take her in his arms. "Surely not. What did that scum do to you, did he hurt you?"

"No—well, yes. I guess he did, but not the way you mean."

"I don't understand."

"He said that—that I'm not—that Matt wasn't my father. That my father was an outlaw who raped my mother and ran off. Oh, Mitch, do you think that could be true?"

"Aw, honey. Aw, dammit, I'm sorry. Don't worry, he's probably lying. He's a worthless piece of crap, that Crane. Even if he is your cousin. Hey, did you ever stop to think, he might be lying about that, too? Being your cousin, I mean."

"It doesn't matter, I killed him. When they find him they'll come after me, too. Do you suppose it's my real father's blood in me and I'm nothing but a killer? Now they're going to be after both of us."

He held her out away from him and studied her tear-stained face. "Don't talk nonsense. You're the same person you always were, Charlie Houston, Matt Houston's daughter, and don't you ever believe any different. And as for running away together, that isn't a good idea. Honey, I've been on the run, I know what it's like. You wouldn't like it one bit, believe me. No, I won't run off with you. Absolutely not!"

"Dammit, we don't have a choice." She jerked from his grasp. "I don't have a choice, and neither do you. There's a reward out for you and now I've committed murder. What do you suggest we do, wait here for them to ride in and shoot us down. Or hang us?"

He chuckled wryly. "They don't usually hang women, especially not women like you. You're well thought of, and Crane Houston is a nobody. They'll believe you when you tell them it was self-defense."

"With Colonel Dunkirk just slobbering for my ranch? No, they won't. That sheriff of his will do just what he wants, and that means they'll send me to jail at best. Mitch, what's wrong with you?"

He shook his head, then took a long look at her. "What's wrong with me is that I love you and I know the value of life, of loving. I'm not going to let this happen to us. I've lost everything I loved once, and dammit I won't let it happen again. We'll figure something out, but we're not running. Not another step. I've run as far as I'm going to, and I sure as hell ain't letting you start."

Frantic, she begged him to listen. But he was acting like a crazy man. Haphazardly packing supplies, throwing things on the table, ranting on about dragging a woman around the country so she could be killed.

He threw a tin cup and plate at the table and both bounced to the floor with a loud clatter. She grabbed his arm and he whirled away from her, but then, as quickly as he had begun the madness, he stopped to stare at the floor, shoulders heaving.

She lay a hand on his back, the shirt soaked with perspiration and clinging to muscles so tense they quivered.

"Please talk to me."

"I can't."

"You have to. I won't leave you, and that's that. And I won't let you leave me either. Say what you want, think what you want. It's not going to happen. No matter what we decide to do, it will be together."

He waited, ramrod stiff, as she moved around him, hands fingering, not losing touch, until she stood squarely in front of him. Head drooping, he swayed as if all energy had been drained from him. She inched up close until their bodies curved together, tried to get him to look at her.

"You're exhausted. You need a lot of rest before you go on. For goodness' sake, you were shot...what, a week ago? Why must we make a decision now?"

He heaved in another breath, pushed past her, and swung open the door. "Then I'll leave, right this minute. If you won't listen to reason, if you won't admit that I know what I'm talking about..."

Conversation abruptly cut off, and he gaped at the thick blanket of falling snow, so dense it had already piled a good foot up against the door. The drift leaked tiny wet puffs onto the floor at his feet.

She ran to stand beside him, then couldn't help but laugh. "Well, go on. Leave."

The words were childlike in their relief. He had no recourse but to remain there with her, indeed, they neither one had any choice but to remain snowbound and together in the cabin.

No one could get to them and they couldn't get out This would give her some time, time to convince him, time to love him. "Oh, look, isn't it beautiful?"

His clenched fists loosened at his side, and he raised his head. "How can you tell?"

You can't see through the stuff."

"Yes, isn't it wonderful?" She put her arms around his waist, laid her head on his chest, and stood there hugging him, until finally his arms lifted and encircled her.

A tired chuckle grew deep in his chest.

"What,? What is it?" "My horse left."

She waited a moment for him to go on, to tell her something amusing. He didn't.

"Mitch, why is that funny?"

He slumped and she felt the weight of his exhaustion.

"I couldn't have left if I'd wanted to. Only a fool would walk in this."

She led him to the small bunk. "Only a fool would even go out in this." She coaxed him to lie down.

He didn't object, just mumbled something about that traitorous Jeb and how he should have known he couldn't trust the crazy horse. "Just like me," he said twice, his voice dying away on the end.

Before covering him to his chin with a blanket she gave him a kiss on lips that responded for a second, then went lax. His breathing evened out and he was asleep instantly. He must have been going on sheer courage alone. The fire crackled pleasantly behind her. For a long time she sat quietly, holding his hand. Then she rose, put on her coat, and plowed her way through the deepening snow to bring in an ample store of wood from the pile Ritter and P.J. had cut and stacked that spring.

The storm swept down out of the mountains, catching the posse far from Miles City and any ranch. They holed up the rest of that day in a stand of lodgepole pine.

Wolf showed up just after dark, lurching into the firelight like some furry animal, scaring the bejeebers out of Ritter. Ritter stared aghast. The last time he'd seen Wolf was when he rode off with Fallon. Where in thunder had he been? And what had happened to Fallon? He wanted to ask, but didn't dare, for fear someone might overhear.

By the following morning the posse found themselves hopelessly snowbound, and it wasn't long before two of the deputies lit out for town, several of Duffy's pals right on their heels.

One declared that making a try for town beat the thunder out of hanging around there getting frostbit or heading off up into those mountains where they'd sure freeze.

McGrew stomped and hollered and turned red in the face till Ritter thought he might bust a gut

Truth to tell Ritter agreed and he told Yancey so, but the ramrod insisted they stick around. "Someone's got to look out for Miss Charlie's interests. If they do run her and Fallon down, I want to be on hand to make sure it goes all right"

"They're gonna shoot that gunslinger, Yancey. You know they are, and no way can we stop 'em," Ritter said.

"Could be, but we can't let them harm Miss Charlie."

"Shooting Fallon will harm her," Ritter muttered, but didn't think Yancey heard him.

At least he made no show of it.

Ritter walked away, then he noticed Wolf standing nearby, close enough to have overheard the conversation.

"He's right, kid," Wolf said in his gravelly voice, startling Ritter for he spoke so seldom. "You need any help, I'm with you. Them two could use an even break, I figger we're it. Don't say nothin', but Fallon's big stallion showed up sometime last night."

Struck speechless, Ritter watched Wolf stride away before he could question him further. The man did talk when he had something to say, but what in the hell could it mean that Mitch's horse was out wandering around? Had the two of them tried to ride out on him and something terrible happened? Things just went from bad to badder, and he felt helpless to do much but watch.

The posse now consisted of Sheriff Newton, Duffy McGrew, a couple of men deputized in town, and four of Duffy's men, plus Ritter, Yancey, and Wolf. There was also, of course, the very unhappy Colonel Hulbert Dunkirk and his unhappier bodyguard, whose name no one had ever heard. The colonel merely summoned the man with a look, when even that much was necessary. It was a mystery where Dunkirk found such loyal servants.

Ritter didn't like it at all, but he wasn't the kind to keep complaining, and besides, he was worried about Miss Charlie. Truth be known, he'd just as soon have had his butt turned to a warm fire back in the bunkhouse of the Double H. It was somewhat consoling that Yancey Barton and Wolf remained for the same reason. The safety of Charlie Houston. Things could be worse, but then they could be a hell of a lot better, too.

Mitch had slept several hours and awakened refreshed if slightly befuddled at their predicament. From where he lay on the uncomfortable bunk he watched Charlie with thinly disguised amazement. She had wound up that music box and was actually cooking, dancing, and humming at the same time. It looked like she had some notion of what she was doing and might be enjoying it. He hated being left with no choices that made sense, but there was a sort of calmness all around, what with the music and Charlie and the knowledge that they were cut off from a world that offered them only a brutal reality.

Brown beans bubbled in an iron pot that hung suspended over the fire. Their rich aroma permeated the small shack. Deftly Charlie stirred up some cornmeal and spooned out the thick batter into cakes on a cast-iron lid shoved onto the coals she'd raked to the front of the fireplace.

Whoever had built the snug line shack had meant its occupants to survive weeks at a time in total isolation. There was food, water, and plenty of firewood.

As if in reply to his wandering thoughts, she interrupted her singing to say, "Thank goodness Yancey had the foresight to have the men build some of these line shacks when we first arrived last year. I was upset at the time he took away from the ranch.

Soon as he had me a cabin, he put up several of these. Said it would mean the difference in life and death for the men caught on the range in bad weather. Now, here it is saving our lives."

Fascinated by her actions rather than her words he barely nodded. "Who taught you to do that?" He pointed toward the johnnycakes puffing in the heat from the coals.

"Last I knew you were living on canned peaches or bumming from the hands' cook fire."

She glanced at him with an embarrassed grin. Her cheeks glowed a rosy red from the fire and a lock of hair tumbled over one eye. A lump rose in his throat. How on God's earth could he leave her?

"Radine—she spent some time with me after you rode out. I asked her to teach me, so I'd make a good wi—" she stumbled, stopped, and stared at him. Her dark, wide eyes filled and she wiped angrily at them with her fingertips.

"Aw, dammit, I'm sorry," he said and held out his arms to her, wincing at the movement. "Come here."

For a moment he thought she wasn't going to move. She held her arms rigid at her sides, her head high and jaw squared like she was daring him. The tough side of her warring against the gentle. Then she reached out and they met, both taking a few steps before going into each other's arms.

"What are we going to do? It makes me want to scream and rant and rave like a madwoman. I waited all my life. All...my... life for someone like you to love. And so now why does it hurt so damn bad I can't draw breath? I swear to you I won't let you ride away from me if I have to hogtie you to that cot over there."

He held her tightly, chin resting on top of her head. "I know, I know. There's a pain, a pain so raw and mean, when I even think of being separated from you. There must be something we can do. Something. Only I just can't come up with it They'll string me up or shoot me if they catch me. And as long as we run somewhere, sooner or later there'll be someone who'll do that. And God only knows what might happen to you."

He sighed. "God, I used to wish he'd come along. The man with the bullet in his gun meant for me. End it all. Stop what was tearing through me like some kind of mad storm. Now, all I can think of, all I want is to go somewhere safe and be with you. In peace. dammit, in peace."

She lifted her tear-stained face and their lips met, their tears mingled.

"Make love to me," she said into his mouth. "Now, and make it last forever."

He slipped his hands under her shirt and caressed the flush of her bare skin, then tenderly lowered her to the floor where he undressed her. Leaning over he saw twin reflections in her black eyes, himself and all he would ever be. Then he slipped out of his clothes and lay beside her, holding her close for a long time before parting her legs and slipping inside.

She cried out once, an ecstatic, sad, happy sound, and then rode with him in silence until they came to a land so far away no one but God and his angels could possibly find them. There they remained for a very long time. Until the fire burned down and the johnnycakes turned dark and crusty, and cold slipped in around the door like a silent thief.

He brought her back as he had taken her, with gentle kisses and the touch of his bare skin on hers. His hair spread upon her breasts, his silken warm lips at the pulse in her throat.

And he didn't know what to do, but he did know that he could never leave this woman and he could not take her with him either. Now he stood on the edge but he wasn't alone, and he no longer wanted to plunge over, not as long as she held so tightly to his hand.

"Charlie," he said finally, the sound of his voice startling them both back to reality. She jerked as if slapped. "I was just dreaming," she said.

"I know, me, too. And I've had an idea."

No reply came, and he lifted to his elbows to study her shadowed face. "You're cold, let me put some wood on the fire." He rose and added a couple of logs behind the cooking food. His bare thighs glistened in the dancing flames and when he turned she saw a glimmer of hope in the fire-lit sheen of his features.

"What is it? Tell me."

"We'll go to Virginia City. I'll give myself up to the marshal."

She sat up, grabbed her shirt, and angrily tried to turn it right side out, not looking at him. "No. No, I won't let you do that!"

"No, listen to me. It was a long time ago, right after the war, maybe I can get amnesty. They did that then. We were outlaws, I reckon, and me the leader. But we never killed. We robbed and shot up some towns. Hell, most of us had no home left to go to. The war ravaged the South. What were we supposed to do? Men like McGrew. Look at him. A successful rancher and a pretty rich wife. He rode with us, too."

Charlie stood there holding her shirt and staring at him. "So that's what he has against you."

"Not just that. The day the posse rode in to round us up, we were having a free- for-all. McGrew and some of his cronies wanted to rob the bank in town. I wanted to stop, go to Canada with my wife, put an end to it all." He shrugged, and tried on a weak grin. "Me and Celia, we got away, they didn't. He spent time in prison, others died. He'd like to get back at me for that."

Thoughtfully she slipped on the garment. "And what about this amnesty thing?

How does it work? Do you think you could qualify?"

"I'll wire my sister Dessa and her husband, Ben. They can help. Amnesty is sort of like a pardon for all your sins, if you promise to go and sin no more. It's because it's easier and cheaper than spending the manpower to chase an outlaw down. Jesse James and Frank, plenty of others were offered pardons, if they'd just quit what they were doing and ride in."

She studied him a moment. She tried not to think of Crane lying in a pool of his own blood, a bullet in him fired from her Winchester. This wasn't about her but about Mitch, who had a bounty on his head. Crane's death might be explained away somehow. "Did any of the outlaws take them up on it?"

He shrugged. "I don't know. I think most of them would rather not. Jesse, he didn't, but I reckon plenty did."

"But you're not up to no good and haven't been, so why would they do that?"

"As far as that lying sheriff tells it, I murdered those two worthless hands of the colonel's. I don't know that I can prove different. I've not committed a foul deed in years, not really. I reckon I could threaten to go back to my outlaw ways if they didn't grant me amnesty."

The attempt at humor fell short and he shrugged.

"I don't know if they would offer me amnesty, but it's worth a try." Excitement colored his tone and he stood on one leg and then the other to put on his pants, talking all the while but not really looking straight at her. "But Dessa and Ben, they have a lot of influence. They own half of northern Montana, railroads, hotels. Everyone respects them. With their help, and the fact that I give myself up and tell them everything... about Yank and all that... well, just maybe it would work."

"And if it didn't?"

He slipped into his shirt and grinned broadly at her. "Well, then I guess you'd just have to bust me out and we'd go on the lam.

We could take up robbing trains and banks, or maybe—" he broke off, losing enthusiasm for his weak attempt to lighten the mood.

Hope surged through her and she answered his grin with one of her own. Maybe, just maybe there was a chance for him. And if there was, she would take her own chances where the killing of her cousin was concerned. Surely, when she told her story about how he had hit her and threatened her, the law would show mercy. What was most important was to free Mitch Fallon once and for all from the cloud of his past. Underneath his brash toughness he was a good and gentle man, and deserved happiness.

They talked and planned into the night, and the next morning, as if the fates had decided to give them at least one chance, a warm wind swept in off the mountains. The snow began to melt. By noon the high drifts were quickly turning to water that rushed down the steep inclines in numerous noisy cascades. The first thing the next morning, they would leave. It would be a long hard trek on foot without Mitch's big black horse. No telling where the beast had gotten to.

Ten

It was pure entertainment, the way the colonel flapped his arms and ranted. Ritter figured if the man didn't stumble head first into a snowdrift soon, he'd have some kind of fit. Yet all he really cared about was seeing that Miss Charlie came out of this with no trouble. With Crane flapping his mouth all the way back to Miles City about her having shot him, that was going to be tough.

Ritter saw McGrew and a couple of his men saddling up and the sheriff, who up to now had been receiving the brunt of the colonel's wrath, including the threat that the man would never be elected in any county in Montana if he didn't catch this outlaw killer, followed suit. The way the warm wind was kicking up off the mountains, this snow would soon be mush and they'd be shedding gear left and right.

McGrew rode his piebald mare right up to the colonel and looked down on him. "Shut up, you old fool. Why don't you git in your fancy little buggy, sir, and ride on back to town. We'll take care of this little problem for you."

The colonel yelled right back. "This little problem is not mine, it is all the good people's of this territory who don't need a bloodthirsty killer riding free."

McGrew glared down at the man, enjoying his advantage.

"Far as I see it, you are the bloodthirsty one, trying to steal all our ranches. Someone ought to hunt you down, same as we're doing to this Fallon, and back-shoot you. That would do the people of this territory a real favor."

The colonel struggled to his feet, fuming until each word sprayed foam. "You mouthy Irish trash, marrying money to get what you want. I ought to run you through."

McGrew tossed back his head and laughed heartily. "Run me through? You old fake. If you ever carried a saber you wouldn't know what to do with one. The closest you've ever come to being in the army is when you run the other way when the conscripters come to town."

Sheriff Newton shoved between the colonel and the mounted man. "McGrew, you don't want to start something here you can't finish. Just look around and use the good sense you were born with."

McGrew glanced to his right where the colonel's big bodyguard stood holding a rifle that could easily blow his head off, and it was pointed right at him.

Colonel Dunkirk began to laugh, an evil sound that chilled Ritter's very soul.

McGrew's reply didn't ease his fears any either.

"You bastard. Someone'll catch you without your hired guns someday and blow you to kingdom come. Solve everyone's problems."

Angrily, McGrew reined his mount aside and joined his cohorts, fuming at them because they didn't back him up. Ritter's attention was caught by the sheriff, who was making an effort to organize the straggly posse.

"Now listen up, men. We're no more than a day's ride from Red Rock Bluffs. If that killer is still holed up there, and he very well may be seein' as how his stallion is here with us, we stop him any way we have to. The bounty don't say he has to be alive, and he's a dangerous man. Biggest chunk goes to the man who guns him down, pure and simple. Now, let's ride."

Miss Charlie was going to get hurt before this was over, Ritter just knew it. He fell in beside Yancey and Wolf, who was leading the big black stallion Jeb, saddled and ready.

The mud was almost worse than snowdrifts. Mitch and Charlie made pretty good time on the rocky trail, but once they reached flat land, their boots sank ankle and calf deep in mire. Each foot sucked up out of the mud carried clumps of the stuff, until the added weight became a burden that slowed their progress. She had insisted on bringing Mitch's rifle, but they carried only the barest of necessities in the way of food, water, and bedrolls. Tucked in her pocket was the deed to the Double H Ranch. The beloved music box was left behind. If they survived, they would come back in the spring and rescue it.

Mitch wore his Colt .44, but even with it on he didn't vaguely resemble the gunslinger she'd first met at spring roundup. He might as well have been someone else, he had changed so much since that day. But then, she supposed she had, too.

Water stood like a lake in the meadow grasses and flowed in furious rivers in every ditch and gully. The sun climbed higher in the sky and they continued to make little progress. As the temperature climbed, their spirits faltered. Sweat made their skin itch and prickle under the woolen underwear and heavy winter clothing both wore. Finally the exertion took its toll on his wounded body and he staggered and went to his knees. She knelt beside him and locked an arm around his waist, afraid he would fall facedown in the snow-crusted water.

"Let's rest awhile," she said. "There's some high ground up under that patch of trees yonder. Can you make it?"

He nodded, stumbled to his feet awkwardly, and together they climbed the rise into the small grove of scraggly pine. With a weary groan, he backed up against one of the scaly barked junipers and slid to the ground on his butt.

"Wet but fine," he said and grinned at her.

The bravery of the gesture made her want to cry. Instead she bit her lip, touched his brow, and found it clammy.

"I'm all right," he said and captured her hand. "Whoo, didn't know I was so wiped out."

"It'd be easier to walk if we kept to the high ground."

He buried his lips in her palm, and she closed her eyes. Oh, God, let this work. Let him be okay. Let nothing happen to him. It was a silent prayer she dared not say aloud, for it would show him how worried she was.

"Not a good idea," he finally said. "There are stretches where there are no trees, no cover at all. If they're out there looking for us we have to stay off high ground, and if that means wading mud and water and snow, then we'll do it. Hell, we don't want to get shot before we can give up, do we?"

"At this rate we're liable to be old and gray before we make it. I think we should circle back to the ranch and get horses. We can wait till dark and sneak in in case they're watching. Ritter and Yancey will help us if we can find them, I know they will."

He held up a hand, signaled for quiet. He shifted around to the other side of the small tree, moved to his knees, and peered out. She stood behind him.

"What?" she whispered.

"There," he said and pointed. "Riders, coming through the gap in those trees at the break of the hill. See?"

She could barely make them out, but he was right. At least

a dozen men rode toward them, their horses struggling through the mud and slush.

"Posse," she said close to his ear. "Vigilantes," he said.

Between them they had only the ammunition in the Winchester and his Colt .44.

Neither carried any spare shells.

She lifted the rifle. He laid a hand across it and pushed the barrel down to point at the ground.

"No more," he said. "No more killing."

"I won't let them take you, even if you will," she said through gritted teeth.

He didn't reply, but continued to watch the riders. If they kept to their present course they would pass within a few hundred yards of where the two of them hid. Maybe they wouldn't see them. It was a slim hope for the small clump of trees offered little cover.

"I have an idea," she said softly. "What?"

"I'll walk out there, give myself up. While they're distracted you drop down the other side of the ridge and make a break for it. They won't shoot me. I'll tell them you got away, went west into the Bighorns. I haven't seen you in days. Not since before the big storm. You got out ahead of it. For all I know you froze to death out there somewhere." She spoke low and fast, all the while preparing to rise and reveal herself.

He didn't say anything for a few seconds as the riders drew closer. Then, "Won't work."

"Yes, yes it will," she practically hissed. "Even if it did, what happens after that?"

She looked at him closely. She couldn't think, her mind was blank. After that? After that he would be alone out here in his weakened condition and she would be alone wherever those men took her, home or jail.

"Whatever we do, we do together, you said so."

Immediately she knew he was right. They had both been too long alone. Whatever their destiny, they would face it together.

At the head of the posse, the leader called a halt. The weary horses hung their heads, some kind of conversation was conducted, and then the riders headed up the rise toward the patch of trees where Mitch and Charlie waited. There was nowhere to hide, and so she took his hand and helped him to his feet.

Then, holding on to each other they stumbled out to meet the approaching posse.

He said to her, almost in jest, "You'd think in country this big they could have ridden another draw, or we could have walked down a mile in the other direction. Then we would have missed each other altogether."

"That's what you'd think, wouldn't you?" she agreed. She wondered if he could feel her trembling.

As Mitch and Charlie approached them, Yancey, Ritter, and Wolf acted in unison.

No secret signal had been exchanged, but it might have been, for they swung their mounts into a barrier between the surrendering couple and the rest of the riders.

McGrew, Sheriff Newton, and the colonel's bodyguard all had their guns cocked and pointed. Scabbards and holsters murmured with the sound of guns being drawn.

Yancey's weapon spoke before anyone could fire, the bullet cut dirt and threw the horses into a crazy hoof-stomping dance.

He shouted at the posse, "They're surrendering, and if you're gonna kill Fallon, you'll have to explain away five bodies." He glanced for confirmation toward his two cohorts and they nodded, grimly keeping their guns aimed.

Sheriff Newton roared, "You sons a bitches. Throw in with that outlaw and I'll put you all on the same scaffold."

"Now, Sheriff," Yancey said, "we're not throwing in with anyone. We're just seeing that things are done fair and square."

"Ain't no fair and square with a killer like Yank. And she went with him, she's painted with the same brush." Newton looked to the colonel and McGrew who nodded in unison.

"You ain't shooting Miss Charlie," Ritter yelled and brought up his rifle.

"Easy, boy," Yancey said out of the corner of his mouth.

A man beside McGrew drew and fired, hitting no target. It was unclear what he had aimed at, but with the crack of the gunshot all hell broke loose.

Mitch threw Charlie to the ground and covered her with his body, at the same time drawing his Colt from the holster. Wolf dismounted and knelt on one knee in front of the fallen couple. He carried an old Sharps and it belched clouds of black smoke and boomed so loud the ground shook.

McGrew's attention never wavered from Fallon. He spurred his mount through the melee of men and screaming horses, intent on only one thing. Killing the man he'd known as Yank. The outlaw leader who had abandoned him and his friends so many years ago. The man who could reveal his own secret identity.

In a flash of memory Mitch recognized the man, and it was as if he had been propelled back to the day at Alder Gulch when his guerrilla band had been attacked and destroyed by Sheriff Moohn outside Virginia City.

The man had been one of the leaders of the revolt within the ranks of Yank's gang—the uprising that had ultimately caused its defeat. Mitch could no longer remember what name he'd gone under, but it hadn't been McGrew. All this flashed through his mind in the instant that McGrew drew bead, and Mitch shouted at Wolf to look out. At the same time he aimed his own Colt and squeezed the trigger. The big .44 shell caught

McGrew in the chest and blew him backward from his saddle, but not before he pulled off his own shot. The bullet slammed into Wolfs arm, spinning him around. The big man let out a grunt, righted himself, and shifted the heavy Sharps to his other hip.

By this time Mitch had struggled to his knees so that he and Wolf formed a solid shield for Charlie. He heard her scrambling around in the mud, muttering her own special curses. But he didn't realize that when he'd thrown her to the ground she'd lost the Winchester, not until he saw from the corner of his eye her making a lunge for the rifle.

He swung around, shouted, "No, Charlie," just as she landed and came up with the Winchester. There she crouched, out in the open with no cover, no protection at all.

Rage twisting his face, the colonel raised his rifle and shot her.

Mitch aimed, fired, and tried to throw himself between her and the deadly bullet, his fevered brain screaming, "Not again," over and over, into a world black and empty. She went down, flying up into the air and landing on her back almost like one of her graceful dances. His ears drummed and darkness closed in upon him, until there was only an endless tunnel and her sprawled in the mud at the end of it. And he couldn't get to her, his feet kept bogging down, and no matter how hard he tried, she was still far away and fading from view.

He heard a tremendous, ungodly roar that he thought was the sound of his heart exploding, his blood erupting, and then he had her in his arms. He didn't realize that the shooting had stopped until much later. All he knew was that the woman he worshiped beyond life itself lay cold and gray and unmoving against his chest, and he had no life, no heart, no love left in him.

She had taken it with her.

Mud plastered her dark hair to one pale cheek, and he

brushed it away tenderly.

She was soaked, her skin icy, and he wrapped his arms around her, held her close, rocked and cried. Someone brought a blanket and wrapped it around both of them.

Voices repeated his name, told him things he didn't want to hear, but he just kept shaking his head, saying, "No, no. Go away and leave us be."

He touched her inert lips with his own. When she didn't respond, he talked to her, told her he loved her, held her against his breaking heart.

Finally words got through to him, oozed into his hearing like tiny echoes from another place and time.

"Let us have her, Fallon. Come on, Fallon, let go."

Enraged, he screamed, "No, you son of a bitch. You've killed her."

But then she jerked in his arms, gasped, made small mewling noises, moaned.

He couldn't believe that it was anything more than his imagination. He breathed her name once, twice, then foolishly, "Is that you?"

Her eyelids fluttered, her lips moved into a wan smile. "My darling, who—else—would—it—be?"

Weak, but alive. She was alive. He sobbed and laughed and held her close. "Let Ritter take her, Fallon. Let's get her to town to a doctor. He'll carry her." "No," he said, glaring ferociously at them and trying to hang on to her.

"You can't even stand, dammit," someone said.

He peered through the haze that still surrounded him, that cut him and his love off from the rest of the world. Hovering there he made out the kid, Ritter.

"I'll carry her myself," he told the boy, but he couldn't get up off the ground with her. What was wrong with him? He wanted to shout to the heavens, "She's alive.

Damn, she's alive," thought he did, but maybe not

Ritter grinned, white teeth gleaming out of a muddy face. "You damn right she is, but if we don't stop all this jawing, she might not be. Now, give her up, man. You've done all you could. You shot the bastard that gunned her. That's your part, now let us do ours."

Ritter touched his shoulder, and Mitch let go the tension and hate and bitterness and fear that had held him together. He allowed Ritter to lift Charlie from his arms, then he remained there a moment fists clenched, head drooping. He no longer held the Colt and had no idea what had happened to it. Trampled in the muck somewhere, he supposed.

Slowly he took in the battle scene. Several bodies lay about on the ground while the men still on their feet loaded the dead and injured belly down on their horses. No one seemed interested in the man they'd been riding out after with such hellacious intent. The leaders were down, wounded, maybe dead. The bodies of McGrew and the colonel were among those being loaded up. The colonel's bodyguard was nowhere to be seen. Perhaps he'd simply ridden away when his boss fell. The sheriff could be one of the bodies so coated in mud as to be unidentifiable. Mitch didn't know or care.

In the midst of it all, in the smoke and the fury and noise, waited the great black stallion. Looking at him, beckoning.

"You son of a bitch, where'd you come from?" he muttered and swayed to his feet.

All he had to do was mount up and ride away. No one would pay him the least attention, nor would they challenge him. The shooting of Charlie Houston had sobered them. Numbly he watched Ritter hand Charlie up to Yancey. The ramrod settled her into his arms and immediately rode off. Ritter and Wolf mounted and followed. He thought about his earlier brief desire to just ride away. It would be the easiest way out for all of them, Charlie included. Someone had saddled the stallion and brought him along. For him, so he could ride away? Everything was a confused mess, and he tried not to think anymore or it might cause his head to burst with the effort. Instead he captured the reins, stepped into the stirrup, and swung onto Jeb's back. Then he touched his heels to the horse's flanks and rode off in the direction that Yancey had taken Charlie. He might not be thinking too well, but he was sure of one thing. He was through running.

Charlie had a bullet in the fleshy part of her backside, the doctor told Fallon when he carried the spent shell over to the jail in Miles City. It had lodged there after plowing through her upper thigh and nicking her hipbone. Doc handed the smashed lead through the bars with a grin and a spark in his brown eyes.

"It'll be more embarrassing than anything else for the little lady. It'll be a spell before she can set down with any ease, and she won't be walking for a while, but everything looks fine. I've put her up at the hotel as we run out of bed space."

Mitch took the misshapen piece of lead. "Thanks, Doc. You sure she's going to be okay?"

The doc grinned. "She's already madder than a cornered bobcat because someone told her you're over here in jail. She's threatened to burn down the town if someone doesn't do something to get you out. With her acting like that, I'd a been here sooner, but had some more patching up to do. Quite a fracas you started out there."

Mitch rolled the lead in his fingers. "I didn't exactly start it, but I think I can finish it. You tell Charlie I've already done just that. My sister and her husband are on their way and they're bringing a newspaper reporter with them. Dessa has telegraphed the governor and Marshal Bracken down in Virginia City.

Bracken'll be riding up, too. Folks jump when my sister hollers, I guess. You tell Charlie everything's going to be just fine. This whole mess will be straightened out real quick.

"Damn, I wish I could see her. Is she really okay? Doc, is there any way she could come see me? They won't let me out of this place."

The doc studied Mitch for a moment, then shook his head. "Not a chance, not for a few days. I don't aim to see that little gal moved, and if she don't quit acting up the way she is I aim to chloroform her or tie her to the bed. Maybe both.

"You just be patient, young man. This'll all work itself out. By the way, how's that shoulder of yours? It looked pretty good when I cleaned it up for you. Bothering you any?"

Mitch flexed the arm and grimaced. "Nah, it's fine. Almost good as new. Now, about Charlie—"

The doc held up his hand. "Don't know which one of you is worse, I'll swear I don't." The doc started out the door, then turned. "Oh, by the way, I've got another fella over there at the hotel who's recuperating, too. Says he's kin to Miss Houston. Goes by the name of Crane Houston. They found him shot out at the Double H a few days ago. He's been kicking up a fuss to see his cousin. I guess I might let him visit with her a bit just to keep her company."

The doctor pulled the door shut behind him.

Mitch stared. What the hell was going on? Charlie said she'd killed that no-good bastard when he tried to..."Hey, Doc," he yelled. "Goddammit, Doc."

The door opened and a young man peered in. "Shut up the blamed caterwauling." "Listen, you've got to take a message for me. Now," Mitch said.

The deputy raised his shoulders in a sigh. "What now, Fallon. I swear you're more trouble than a cell plumb full of

Saturday night drunks."

"This is important."

"Of course it is."

"Go to the doc's place and tell him whatever he does not to let Crane Houston anywhere near Charlie. You tell him that, now, you hear?"

"You mean that fella we found shot out at the Double H?"

"That's who I mean. Now, go, dammit! It fact, you take a pair of handcuffs and you put them on that no-good son of a bitch. You arrest him. He tried to—I mean, he wants to steal the Houston ranch."

"Aw, dang, I can't do that"

Fallon ground his teeth. "Where the hell's the sheriff?" "We ain't got us no sheriff."

"What happened to Sheriff Newton?"

"You got me."

"And just who are you?"

"Name's Acorn and no cracks."

"Is he dead?"

"Who?"

Mitch gritted his teeth. "The sheriff."

Acorn studied Fallon a minute. "Now why the hell would you ask me that? Of course, he ain't dead. I don't reckon. He rode off, said they didn't pay him enough to fool with the likes of you and all your friends. Now this town don't have any law."

"I want to see Ritter and Yancey. Right now," he roared at the deputy, who had continued to ramble on about the sorry fate of the town.

"Don't get your hide all stretched out of shape. I'll find them, anything to get you to shut up."

"And you'd better get over to the hotel and watch Crane Houston, if you don't want me to wring your scrawny neck right through these bars." Filled with frustration and helplessness, Mitch kicked the slop bucket clear across the cell, spilling its contents all over the dirty floor. He immediately regretted that.

"Now look what you've gone and done," Acorn yelped. "Dear God, will you do what I told you to?"

"I'm going, I'm doing it" the deputy said, and backed out the door, face screwed up against the offensive odor coming from Mitch's cell.

Ritter sat beside Charlie, twisting his hat round and round in nervous fingers. She peered closely at him. "You're sure it's over? I mean, the whole thing?" "Colonel Dunkirk is dead, ma'am." He grinned at her expression, but went on without apology. "McGrew was wounded, and they've sent him to Denver to be with his wife. Where he shoulda been in the first place, if you want to know what I think. The bounty has been removed off Fallon's head for gunning Cross and Neddy, Sheriff Newt had a knot on his head the size of a goose egg and was so mad when he came to riding belly down on his horse that he resigned as soon as he got back to town and rode off God knows where. Course everyone knows it was really 'cause he no longer had the colonel to protect his job. The whole town is in an uproar, trying to come up with someone they can vote in as sheriff before the marshal arrives from Virginia City and lots of 'em are saying Wolf would be just fine if he'd—"

"Whoa, Ritter. Wait a minute. Why is Mitch still in jail?"

"Well, ma'am, he—I mean, the telegram from the marshal ordered us to—well, to hold him till he gets here. Something about his actions after the war. Why, did you know he was as famous as Quantrill? Led a band of marauders just the same as him, guerrillas, they say."

"And the marshal is going to send him to prison for something that happened ten years ago?"

Ritter shrugged. "I don't know. All we know, Yancey and me, is that we're under strict orders from a U.S. Marshal, and we can't go agin them, now can we?"

Charlie sighed. "I suppose not, but dammit, Ritter, he doesn't belong in jail. Hasn't he been through enough without this? I want to see him, make sure he's all right. I can't stand just laying here like this."

Doc came in then and chased Ritter off.

The doc pivoted, the brown bottle of laudanum in one hand and a glass of water in the other. "I got someone in the other room who wants to see you as soon as you're up to it. Says he's your cousin. A fella by the name of Crane Houston?"

"That's not possible, he..."

"Are you all right? You look pale as ashes. My word, child."

Charlie gasped, clung to the bedcovers as the room revolved crazily. She swayed, her mouth went dry, then filled with saliva that choked her.

Doc let the laudanum and water glass clatter to the bedside table and wet a cloth to press to her forehead. "You've had too much excitement, that's all," he soothed. "Now just relax. I'll give you this and you can sleep. There's nothing to worry about."

"No, no. You don't understand." Why wouldn't he listen? The man she thought she had killed lay in the next room, obviously quite alive, and this man refused to listen to what she had to say.

He poured a measure of liquid into the water and held it to her lips until she drank.

She sipped and swallowed, frightened eyes wide and pleading, until the glass was empty.

"Now calm down, go to sleep."

"Don't let anyone in here, please," she said through numb lips. "Don't let him—" Gentle darkness crept over her like blankets of thick wool, and the fear oozed away.

Eleven

Radine glared down at Ritter and Yancey, slamming down their mugs of beer so that the foam sloshed all over the table.

"You men are always up to some orneriness that nearly gets women folk hurt. You never can just let things go along and work themselves out." She paused a minute, but not long enough for either of them to reply. "Course, all I really care about is that Charlie is going to be okay."

The three broke out in wide grins and the two men sipped their beers for a while in silence.

Instead of leaving and tending to her other customers, Radine leaned on the table and ogled Ritter. He gazed openly at her breasts pushed up by a corset so that the blush of her nipples peeked out at him. He was beginning to feel pretty randy, now that everything was done and settled, and he toyed with asking Radine to go to a crib with him. The idea crawled around in his groin and he shifted in the chair.

She winked at him, but what she said didn't match her actions. "Hear about Red Cloud and Sitting Bull?"

"No," Yancey said. "They finally get the savages?"

"That ain't all. After Crook attacked at Slim Buttes and American Horse surrendered, Red Cloud's bunch was disarmed. Army took their horses and guns."

"Well, dang!" Yancey said. "Well, ain't it about time?"

She took a deep breath and went on. "Then Colonel Miles followed old Sitting Bull to Cedar Creek and him and all them Sioux just flat surrendered. Some say there were thousands of them."

"Soldiers?" Ritter asked. "No, Indians."

"Aw, bull. The army defeated thousands of Sioux? I don't believe that." "Well, it's true," she said, hand in the air for emphasis. "I heard it from some soldiers themselves."

She blushed and fiddled with a little bow ribbon between her breasts. Once again, Ritter's glance skittered into place there.

She ran her hand down his arm, and he gulped audibly. She whispered in his ear, "I got some things I could teach you."

He slammed the empty beer mug down and kicked back his chair. She giggled, touched her red hair, and led Ritter toward the stairs.

Charlie hitched one eye open, felt the bed spin, and groaned. Her stomach roiled. Crane was in the next room. What would he do to her when he recovered enough to move around? She had to get away from this place before he did. He was supposed to be dead, killed by the bullet from her rifle. Well, at least she didn't have to worry about being arrested for his murder. Still, he must have told someone who had shot him. Why hadn't anyone said anything?

Her head cleared and she remembered Crane's threat with more clarity, the ace up his sleeve he'd spoken about. Something he claimed would prove she was not Matt Houston's daughter, and therefore not his legal heir. What could it be? She had to find out, and if she couldn't walk, then she would crawl. After everything that had happened, she would not lose the ranch, too. She would be there when Mitch was set free, no matter how long it took. He would have a home to come back to.

Her heart ached with loneliness and despair. How would she stand it if they sent him away to prison?

A familiar voice interrupted her thoughts, and she clutched at the mattress when she rolled her head on the pillow and saw Crane Houston leaning heavily against the door frame and grinning with all the evil he had in him.

"Well, well, lookee who's here." He shuffled toward her.

Charlie stared at her cousin in the open doorway as if he were a coiled snake. The pain in her hip grew more intense. She suppressed an urge to leap from the bed, rake at his eyes, seeing as how she couldn't move. The animosity of his ugly grin told her he'd not come to inquire after her health.

She shifted, tried to lift the injured leg with both hands and work her way to the edge of the mattress. Face him on her feet. Sweat beaded her forehead, and she felt giddy, finally gave up on the impossible task and lay back against the pillows. Her gown was drenched, her hair hung in wet strands that clung to her face and neck, and she was totally exhausted by the effort. Not once during the ordeal did she move her gaze from the man in the doorway.

He looked about as drained as she felt but managed to take several shuffling steps toward her, one arm wrapped around his right side. Without the door facing to support him it appeared as if he might fall at any moment, but he made it to the foot of the bed and leaned there breathing heavily.

At last she could croak out some words. "What do you want?"

"You shot me."

She sent a quick look toward the door. The hallway was empty, quiet. "I thought you were dead."

He nodded, fingered around in the pocket of a loose robe he wore over pajamas, came out with a folded square of newspaper. "See what you think of your folks now, cousin," he sneered and skimmed the paper in her direction. It floated onto the coverlet just within her reach.

For a long while she just stared at the offering. It would be best if she didn't read it, but there was no way she could manage that. And so she stretched her arm out, leaned forward until she could pinch the clippings between two of her fingers.

"Get out of here," she told him.

"No. I want to see your face when you find out all about your real daddy and his whore. Read it, go ahead. And then I'll leave." He stopped and took several breaths. She could tell he was in a great deal of pain, but felt no compassion for him.

Licking her dry lips she began to unfold the small square of yellowed newsprint.

After pacing what seemed like a hundred miles in the tiny cell, Mitch was relieved to be interrupted by the sound of the outside door opening and closing. He hoped to see someone with a message from Charlie, but it was the young deputy Acorn.

"Did you tell the doc—?" Mitch didn't finish the question before Acorn interrupted him.

"Someone's here to see you." The deputy's eyes bugged, as if he didn't quite believe his own announcement. "It's Mr. and Mrs. Ben Poole. They're right outside, and there's this reporter fella with them. He says he's going to write all about you. How you were a hero in the war and afterward your whole family thought you were dead, only you were really an outlaw trying to right the wrongs of the..."

A tall blond gentleman filled the doorway behind the deputy and interrupted the tirade with a hearty laugh. "Mitchell Fallon, I thought we'd never see your ornery hide again. Have to confess, though, I'd have figured you to be behind bars when I did. How in the world are you, anyway? I've got someone here who's just dying to see you."

Ben Poole turned without waiting for a reply, took the arm of Mitch's sister Dessa, and pulled her through the doorway.

Green eyes met matching green eyes and Mitch extended his arms through the bars in an attempt to hug his tall, beautiful sister. "Oh, God, it's good to see you. How are you? You look wonderful. How was your trip? Damn, it's good to see you."

Dessa laughed delightedly and reached through the bars, too, so that they were hugging even with the unyielding iron between them. "We've missed you so much. How could you go away for so long and only write twice? I was so sorry to hear about Celia and the baby. What a tragedy.

"But we're all here now and together again. You've gotten yourself in quite a fix, haven't you? When are you going to settle down like the rest of us?"

Mitch stared at Dessa. How lovely and elegant she looked, not at all like the young girl who had ridden off to make her fortune with an equally young Ben Poole.

He beamed at her, despite all his worries about Charlie. "I'm ready, truly ready. I swear if I get out of this mess I'm going to spend the rest of my life just behaving myself."

Ben laughed uproariously. "That'll make the law happy."

The shy, soft-spoken, and gentle young man Mitch remembered had certainly changed. Despite his self-assurance and sophisticated demeanor, though, Ben still eyed Dessa in that hauntingly adoring way Mitch remembered.

"Well," Mitch said, "what's this about some reporter?"

"That's James Magruder, the fella with the pencil glued to his hand." Ben indicated a studious man with thinning hair and a round, childish face that lit up when Mitch nodded in his direction.

Ben went on. "You two will have plenty of time to talk later. First, let's see what we can do about getting you out of here."

"They told me I had to stay until the marshal arrived from Virginia City," Mitch said.

"That's ridiculous." Dessa lifted her skirts and swept past Ben to hail an enraptured

Acorn, who had squeezed his way back into the outer office but still gaped in awe at the impressive visitors. "Young man. Yes, you. Kindly bring the keys to my brother's cell. He has business to attend to and it can't be carried out in this filthy jail cell. And please get someone to clean this place up, it stinks."

Acorn grinned and nodded, then grinned some more.

Then Mitch thought again of Charlie's predicament, and his ensuing outburst drew everyone's attention. "My God, we have to do something about Charlie."

Deputy Acorn came through the door, amazingly offering a key to the cell. Mitch addressed him. "Did you talk to Doc?"

"About what?" the young man asked, wearing his usual befuddled expression. "Dammit, I sent you to check on Charlie and that no-good—you remember, I told you about Crane Houston. Unlock this damn door. Now!"

Ben grabbed the key, stuck it in the lock, and swung the door open all in one efficient motion. Mitch remembered that about him. He never wasted time on useless questions.

"Come on, come with me. Everyone," Mitch yelled as he ran from the sheriffs office out into the street. "That son of a bitch better not have harmed a hair of her head."

"Oh, I can see you've really changed, brother," Dessa called, but again hiked up the skirt of her expensive silk dress to hurry after him. Ben, Magruder, and Acorn brought up the rear.

Mitch busted through the door of the hotel without bothering with the usual amenities. An elderly woman seated in the lobby huddled into her chair and stared wide-eyed at his entourage mounting the stairs. At the top he paused only a second after spotting four doors along the hallway. The first one on the left stood open to reveal Crane and Charlie.

Startled, both turned an amazed gaze toward him. Charlie's lovely dark eyes were awash with tears.

"You son of a—" Mitch headed for Crane, intent on mayhem. Ben and Dessa grabbed his arms, held him back.

For a fraction of a second everyone remained frozen in place, then Mitch shook loose and went to Charlie, touched her, half turned to make another grab at Crane. "What'd you do to her, you thieving piece of—"

Crane cowered backward, whimpered. "No, Mitch, no," Charlie said. "Don't."

Latecomers Magruder and Acorn crowded into the room.

"Why not? Give me one good reason why I shouldn't wipe up the floor with this worthless piece of... what's that?" He pointed at the newspaper clipping.

She ignored the last question. "Because I love you and he's worthless, but you aren't. Please, Mitch. Let's just let it all be over."

Dessa clamped his arm tighter. "Listen to her and don't go off half-cocked. Remember where you've just been."

For Mitch, when Charlie professed her love in front of everyone, it was as if his wild intent to do Crane bodily harm slammed up against a rock wall. Loving her would prevent him continuing in the direction in which he'd been aimed all these years. He would have to turn and face up to reality, take a hand in his own destiny. Though his inclination had been to choke the life out of the little runt hanging over the foot of the bed, all he really wanted was to be with Charlie.

Taking another look at the pitiful Crane Houston, he figured the man might die on his own without any help from anyone.

Mitch extended his hands, palms down. "Okay, I won't kill him. Not yet, anyway." He turned in disgust from the lowlife to concentrate on Charlie who looked pretty peaked. He wiped tears from her cheeks with his thumbs.

"God, how I've missed you," he said and kissed her gently, once, twice, then yet again but with much more intensity.

She sighed, reached for him, then let herself go limp in his arms. "Who are all these people staring at me? Can't we go away somewhere and be alone? Oh, Mitch, you should read this. It's—it's just so... sad." She broke into great racking sobs.

He held her until the sobbing faded. After she came to her senses, wiped her face, and apologized to her visitors, Ben took over.

"I'm Ben Poole, Mitch's brother-in-law. This is my lovely wife, Mitch's sister Dessa, and this young man scribbling frantically is the fellow who will help see that Mitch doesn't go to jail, James Magruder. And back there, peering in like a hooty owl, that's the only law this poor town has to offer at the moment. Afraid I didn't catch the young fellow's name."

"Acorn," Mitch muttered and patted Charlie to reassure himself she was real and okay.

She caught his hand fiercely and nodded up at the blond giant, then her ebony eyes searched out Mitch's gaze once again. She held up the newspaper clipping without saying a word.

"Aw, don't cry. It's not good for you. You have to get well."

"I—am—well. I just—oh, dammit to hell, Fallon, read that."

Dessa gasped and Mitch couldn't suppress a slight chuckle. The old Charlie was surfacing, despite everything she'd been through lately.

He moved to the window to read. There was no sound in the room except for an occasional sniffle from Charlie. Both Dessa and Ben tried to comfort her while Acorn quietly escorted a protesting Crane Houston from the room.

El Grande, Texas, June 15. A most heinous crime was committed in this small quiet community Tuesday when the fifteen-year-old daughter of the prominent Hernando Florez family was kidnapped and violated by three notorious Texas bandits. According to Sheriff Clark the men abducted Miss Dolores Florez as she strolled about the grounds of her family's hacienda. They shot and wounded three servants in their escape with the young girl. Miss Florez was found unconscious in a shack some fifteen miles from town the next morning. Doctor Northrup stated that with rest and care she will recover.

Mitch glanced at Charlie and she nodded miserably. Every time she closed her eyes she saw her poor mother, herself a mere child, fending off those horrible men.

Mitch went back to reading.

Sheriff Clark reports the men who committed the dastardly deed are still at large. A bounty of $500 has been placed on the head of each of the outlaws, dead or alive.
Posters are on display prominently around town.

Mitch frowned. Clearly, this proved to Charlie what her cousin had claimed, that she was not the child of Matt Houston, but of some low-life bandit. She would be able to count back from the date of her own birth and figure it out.

He only wanted rid of the entire matter. While he might understand how this could make her feel, it made no difference to him at all where their lives were concerned.

To show her so, he wadded the newspaper clipping into a tiny ball and tossed it in a bin near her bed, then sat gingerly beside her. Holding her hand in his he studied her drawn features.

"What is it, Charlie? Are you feeling worse? None of this means anything to us, nothing at all."

She gulped air as if she were drowning. Emotions choked her. Since her father's death she had never really allowed herself to break down and mourn. Now that she had more to grieve than his death, it was as if she couldn't stop crying. Matthew Houston was not her father. He had lied to her all those years. How could she ever reconcile such betrayal? She was truly some bandit's bastard child.

She clung to Mitch's hand, gazing at the way their fingers gripped. She couldn't meet his gaze.

"Darlin', none of this matters. All I care about is you and me, us, together always.

This, it means nothing. Matthew Houston loved you and that's all you need to remember. You are his daughter, more truly than any of this. Otherwise, he'd have left you." He spoke softly but urgently. "You're tired now. We'll leave, let you get some rest. But wouldn't you stop crying, or at least tell me why you're so upset."

"No, don't go. Stay a few minutes. We need to talk, and I'm fixing to shut up this bawling. It's pretty undignified." She wiped her face on a corner of the sheet and Ben passed her a large white handkerchief.

"We need to get to our hotel and freshen up," Dessa said quickly. "James, you come with us if you don't mind. There'll be plenty of time to get your story when the marshal arrives."

Dessa swept from the room, shooing everyone ahead of her, including Acorn who had returned to hover outside the door. He murmured a mild protest, but it did him no good. Dessa Poole was in charge.

Mitch grinned toward the closed door, then turned back to Charlie. "Now, what's going on here? This isn't like you at all. A woman who rides herd on a bunch of ornery cows after being caught in the middle of a stampede doesn't let much get her down."

Charlie didn't know where to begin. With trembling fingers she touched Mitch's face, grazed their tips over the scar that cut through his eyebrow to the white streak of hair. A forever reminder of his own tragic loss. "Oh, Mitch, I do love you so. But I'm afraid."

"Of me? I'm sorry. You've nothing to be afraid of. I know I get pretty stormy—"

She touched his lips, shushing the words. "No, not that. *That.*" With a slight movement of her head she indicated the receptacle in which he'd thrown the clipping.

"What does that—"

"I'm trying to get up the nerve to tell you, but I'm afraid you'll hate me, or be so disgusted you'll just walk away."

"Aw, hell, Charlie. Nothing could make me leave you now. Nothing in the whole wide world. I'm finished with running away, especially from you." He leaned over and kissed first her forehead, then each eye before trailing his warm, moist lips down her jaw-line to her throat, then up along her chin to her mouth.

She tasted of his precious love, afraid that this would be the last time he offered it The thought emptied a great hole within her and the pain seared far worse than the bullet that had torn through her flesh. "Oh, Mitch. Mitch, please love me."

He trailed his fingers over the flannel gown and cupped her breast so that his thumb brushed the nipple. "I do, darlin', but we can't right now. Not here. It'll wait till we marry."

She crooned down in her throat, and he silenced the sound once again with his lips.

He realized that his greatest fear had been that she would not marry him or that something would happen to her. Now here she was expressing a like fear over some damned old yellow newspaper clipping that dated back twenty-five years or more. No matter what it proved, it didn't matter to him, and he wished with all his heart that it didn't matter to her either. He loved her. Yet he could tell that until she explained she would never be free of whatever awful burden she carried.

He pulled reluctantly away from the kiss, cupped her face with one hand. Although from what little she'd told him he could pretty well figure it out, he sensed she needed to talk about the past and lay it to rest.

"Okay, tell me, now, and then we'll forget all about it."

"Do you promise?"

"Oh, yes. I promise."

And so she told him everything. How her father had come for her when she was a child after her mother killed herself. How her grandparents had let her go because she reminded them of her mother's shame.

"I'm a bastard. I thought Matt Houston was my father. All those years of calling him Daddy and loving him, and all the time some dirty, murdering bandit sired me in a filthy shack. A man who doesn't even know I exist and wouldn't care if he did. And even my mother probably didn't know which one of them fathered me."

Mitch rubbed at her temple with a thumb. "None of that was your fault or your mother's, or even your... I mean Houston's fault."

"But he lied to me. I wasn't his daughter and I loved him so much. He could have told me the truth."

"And what would he have said? He probably didn't know what to tell you when you were a child, then when you grew up he just loved you so much he didn't think it mattered. He was your father, Charlie, in every way. Don't you see that?"

"But Crane said he was taking money from my grandparents all along. That's how he bought the ranch. If he truly loved my mother and me he wouldn't have taken money to raise me," she said. Anger had replaced tears and he thought that a good sign.

"You only have Crane's word for that. All that clipping proves is that your poor mother endured a horrible experience. You may have been conceived before your parents married, I guess you could tell that from the dates. But on the other hand, you may have been born early, or your mother and father might have—well—had a little fun out back in the barn. Be realistic, none of the rest of the story is anything but that filthy man's lies, and I won't have him hurt you like this anymore. I'll kill him, Charlie. I swear I will."

Frantic, she grabbed at his arms. "No. No, don't do that. They'll put you back in prison. He has to stay alive. Oh, God, if I had killed him I'd be in jail right now. Oh, Mitch, hold me."

He gathered her close and she nestled into the curve of his embrace. "Don't talk nonsense. He attacked you and you defended yourself. No one would ever have put you in jail for that. We talked about this before."

"What will happen to him now? Can he claim the ranch as my father's—Matt's only heir?"

Mitch's eyes shimmered with rage. "Let him try. It'll do no good at all. He has no real proof. When I get through talking to him I believe he'll be glad to get away from Montana Territory with his scalp and hide intact."

"Don't you dare do anything else to get in trouble."

"Don't you worry. Now, close your eyes and go to sleep. I'll just sit in yonder chair awhile and watch over you."

She smiled and it felt good. Never had she thought she would be happy to let a man watch over her... never had she thought that man would be Mitchell Fallon. Things certainly had a strange way of working out.

Twelve

Doc allowed Mitch to move Charlie that evening.

He took her gently in his arms and carried her down the hallway where Ben and Dessa Poole met him in the doorway of a large suite of rooms. Yancey and Ritter came along because neither was willing to completely release Miss Charlie to the care of this reformed gunslinger who had stepped in and taken over her life.

Dessa and Ben insisted that Charlie take the larger of the two suites they had rented. There was an adjoining but separate room for Mitch.

Yancey eyed Ritter and he returned the wry look. Wasn't this just too cozy? Miss Charlie and that outlaw separated only by a thin door. Ritter figured he shouldn't be too surprised, seeing as how they had been together alone in that line shack for so long. He thought seriously about riding out for Idaho Territory and finding him a job in some bar where he could drink away his woes and be spared watching Miss Charlie make a complete goggle-eyed fool out of herself.

Yancey muttered as they left the room, "Reckon she's too good for him, but what do we know?"

"I got me an idea," Ritter said. "Let's go over to the Powder Keg and have a few more beers."

It was going to take a heap more than a few beers to get him over loving Miss Charlie.

"I got a better one," Yancey said. "Let's ride to Virginia City and file claims on all that land Dunkirk has that's just going to waste before someone else beats us to it."

Ritter stopped in the middle of the hallway and stared at Yancey. "You mean start our own spreads?"

"Or throw in with Miss Charlie and Fallon. Whatever works. Hell, maybe we can build our own dynasty and do it fair and square without killing anyone."

Ritter grinned great big and followed Yancy from the hotel, slapping the Stetson on his head as he went outside.

After the door closed behind them, Mitch said, "Somehow I don't like the idea of you two putting us up. We can take care of ourselves."

"Oh, don't worry," Dessa said, green eyes sparkling like she had some gigantic secret. "It's your money that'll pay for this suite. We can't let the half-owner of the P & F Railroad and the Great Montana/Dakota hotel chain sleep in just any old room."

Mitch plunked down beside Charlie on the large overstuffed divan where he'd carefully placed her. "What exactly are you talking about? You and Ben own..."

His sister began shaking her head and laughing.

"She insisted on investing your money in it, too," Ben said. "I told her she should ask, but she just took your half of the inheritance and smacked it right in there with ours. God knows how she would have explained it to you had we gone bust." Ben joined his wife in laughter.

"What are they talking about?" Charlie asked.

"I have no idea," Mitch said. "I had no money, no inheritance...."

Dessa leaned forward in her chair. "Oh, yes you did.

Daddy never gave up looking for you. He believed you were alive and he left half of everything to you in that event. I'm sorry I gambled with it. I do hope you'll forgive me. You're rich, Mitchell. Aren't you happy?"

He stared at Dessa, then at Ben, and finally down at Charlie, who looked as astounded as he felt. "But... but... I can't take—"

"Nonsense, of course you can. We'll never miss it, honestly. Besides, we've been very careful in our accounting, and your share of the profits is in your name in a trust. We couldn't touch it if we wanted to. The capital, now that's another matter, and one Ben handles.

"Of course, if you want to continue the investment and just draw on your profits, Ben has some wonderful ideas for expanding westward in the near future. In fact, we're on our way to California when we leave here."

"I'm not a businessman," Mitch protested. "I'm a..."

He broke off.

What was he? For years he'd been a wanted man, an outcast, an outlaw, a gunslinger. How did that fit into this new turn of events? And suppose the marshal from Virginia City decided to arrest him and put him in jail for the rest of his life. What then?

He turned once again to the woman he loved. "Charlie?"

She peered up at him. All she wanted this very moment was to be alone with the man she loved in their own home.

Mitch pressing her hand in his. "We'd better wait until we hear what the marshal has to say before we make any plans."

Dessa squirmed, a little of the young sister Mitch remembered passing across the sophisticated features. In a soft voice she said, "He's coming to offer you amnesty, just like you wanted. The governor authorized it, in fact insisted upon it."

Charlie gasped, dread evaporating like river mist on a summer morning. "Oh, it can't be true."

"Yes," Dessa said. "It is true. There'll be some compensation to be paid. You did rob some people, Mitch, and even if you felt justified because of what happened in the war, you'll have to pay it back."

"How in the world did you manage that?" Mitch asked.

Dessa's green eyes, like a reflection of his own, flashed through lowered lashes. "I told the governor how embarrassing it would be to have the hero of James Magruder's novels languishing in jail. That bright young man has a publisher interested in what he'll write about you. You behave now and tell him some good stories, will you? Not anything that will embarrass the fine family name. I convinced both the governor and Marshal Bracken that it would be better this way, for everyone."

Ben slapped his leg and laughed. "A little gentle blackmail never hurts."

Mitch stared at the window. Outside, lamps flickered on all over town, little pinpoints of yellow light like beacons in the falling darkness.

He thought of all the men he'd killed during the war, and how oftentimes what came afterward was a war of sorts, too. That was certainly forgivable when it couldn't be helped, wasn't it? Was it possible, though, that the law would give him another chance?

The Colt he'd carried still lay buried in the mud somewhere out there in the foothills of the Bighorn Mountains, and it could stay there for all he cared.

"Mitch?" Charlie said. "Are you all right?"

He turned from the window. Her dark eyes reflected the points of light from outside and telegraphed to him so much love that he felt wrapped in it, warmed and protected forever. That other life belonged to someone else, someone he no longer even knew.

"I think we'll build a house out at the Double H, if it's all right with Charlie," Mitch said after a long silence. "I think we'd both be happy living out there."

Charlie stared at him, filled with a love so genuine and sensual she could scarcely speak. "And Yancey and Ritter can run it for us when we want to travel."

Mitch, Ben, and Dessa all laughed.

"Sounds like she's got the right idea. Believe me, it doesn't take long to get used to having money," Ben said.

Dessa smiled and touched her husband's cheek. "I can remember when Ben didn't have anything but a blanket and a beat-up old rifle. And look at him now."

Ben hugged his wife. "Yeah, just look."

"And when will you two get married?" Dessa asked from the comfort of her husband's arms.

The question brought another laugh from everyone. "As soon as I can walk down the aisle," Charlie said.

Mitch took her hand and brought it to his lips. "Why wait till then? I can always carry you."

A little over a week later, on a beautiful and crisp Saturday afternoon in early November, Mitchell Fallon and Charlie Houston were married in the small church in Miles City.

A disgruntled Crane Houston sat behind the bars of the jail where acting Sheriff Wolf Springer had put him when Marshal Bracken announced the man was wanted all over the territories for fraud of various kinds. He might truly be Charlie's cousin, as he'd claimed, but he was definitely the black sheep of that family. Probably the reason Matthew Houston never mentioned his name to either his beloved daughter or his friend and ramrod Yancey Barton.

By this time Charlie truly believed that her father had loved her. It was tough to forgive him for his deception, but she thought she understood. As Mitch kept telling her, forgiving was easy when you loved someone enough.

"At least I certainly hope so." He gazed at her with a familiar gleam in his shining green eyes and rested his hands at her waist.

She put her arms around his neck. Of course he was right.

Determined to walk down the aisle, she and Yancey practiced every day until she could manage the short stroll without stumbling.

On her wedding day Wolf lifted her from the carriage that brought her and Yancey to the church and carried her as far as the entrance. Then he stood in the center of the street, a sheriff's star gleaming on his chest, and watched Marshal Therm Bracken ride out of town to the strains of the wedding march. Then he slipped silently into the church.

Charlie ignored twinges of pain and tried not to limp as she and Yancey started down the aisle. Through glimmering tears she looked from Dessa Poole, her dark beauty stunning in peach organza, to her husband Ben in silver-striped trousers and morning coat, and then finally to Mitchell Fallon who wore black trousers, a boiled white shirt, and a waistcoat that he looked ready to tear off at any moment.

There hadn't been time to get fancy clothing for the wedding, but Charlie wore a stunning cream silk-and-lace dress that belonged to Dessa and had been altered for her smaller build. A cloud of organza cascaded around her shoulder-length dark hair.

Mitch caught his breath as Yancey brought his bride to him, then hid a smile behind his hand when he noticed the tips of her riding boots peeking from beneath the hem of the dress. Just like Charlie not to wear the white slippers. He'd never tame this one, but he didn't mind at all. She was his Charlie, wild and a little stubborn, but for a man like him that was perfect.

He accepted her hand, tucked it firmly into the crook of his elbow, and together they faced the preacher.

THE END

Velda Brotherton writes from her home perched on the side of a mountain against the Ozark National Forest. Branded as *Sexy, Dark and Gritty*, her work embraces the lives of gutsy women and heroes who are strong enough to deserve them. After a stint writing for a New York publisher, she has settled comfortably in with small publishers to produce novels in several genres.

Facebook: Author Velda Brotherton
Twitter: @veldabrotherton
www.veldabrotherton.com